PHANTOM

SILVER SAINTS MC

FIONA DAVENPORT

Copyright © 2023 by Fiona Davenport

Cover designed by Elle Christensen.

Edited by Editing4Indies

All rights reserved.

No part of this book may be reproduced in any form or by any electronic or mechanical means, including information storage and retrieval systems, without written permission from the author, except for the use of brief quotations in a book review.

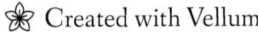 Created with Vellum

PHANTOM

Kian "Phantom" Weber spent fifteen years working in the shadows to protect his country. The retired spook found his family with the Silver Saints MC... and they eventually led him to the woman who was meant to be his.

When Phantom spotted the bruises on Tessa McGuire's arm, he knew he would burn down the world to ensure her safety. With him at her side, anyone who wanted to hurt Tessa would have a battle on their hands. Because he knew in an instant that he'd have her back. Always.

1

TESSA

I hadn't been expecting a call from my bank, so I assumed the representative would try to sell me something. I was only paying half attention until she said, "I'm sorry, but we cannot process your withdrawal request because none of the boxes were checked for the reason for the distribution. You'll need to send in a new form with all the sections completed."

My brows drew together as I tilted my head to the side. "I'm sorry, what?"

After repeating the information, the person from the bank added, "Or you can submit the request online if you need the funds more quickly. Also, please note that pulling all the funds from the account will result in its closure. And you should be aware that if this is a non-qualified distribution, the amount will be subject to income tax and a 10 percent penalty."

"I think you misunderstood my question. I'm not sure what you're talking about because I didn't send in a withdrawal request."

"But I have it right here." I heard some shuffling of papers in the background. "And the signature appears to match what we have on file for you."

My mom had squirreled a lot of money away into that account to ensure I could attend college without having to worry about paying for it. Earning a degree wasn't that important to me, except that it was the best way to get away from the town where I grew up. My childhood had been fairly normal...until my mom passed away in a car accident last year. Then my dad turned into a completely different person.

The father who'd taught me how to ride a bicycle and took me to the park every weekend was long gone. In his place was someone my mom would've hated. Especially with how he neglected me.

The only upside to her being gone was that she wasn't here to see how far he'd fallen. Especially if he'd done what I was starting to suspect.

"Ahh, yeah. Thanks for calling to let me know there was an issue. I'll take care of it on my end."

I ended the call before she could ask how I'd forgotten I sent in paperwork to withdraw almost sixty-thousand dollars. Unfortunately, that wasn't quick enough for my dad to come into the living room and catch the tail end of my conversation.

"Who was that? What issue were they calling about?"

Setting my cell on the cushion beside me, I took a deep breath before answering. "Someone from the bank letting me know that the form to empty my college savings account was missing a checkmark in a section, so they couldn't process it."

"Shit," he muttered, stomping closer.

"The funny thing is that I never sent in the request." I pressed my lips together as I glared up at him. "But you know that already, don't you?"

"I need that money," he growled, reaching out to grab my arm. Gripping hard, he yanked me off the couch.

"Oww," I cried, feeling as though my shoulder was being wrenched out of the socket.

He hissed, "I need that money, and you're gonna get it for me."

I blinked up at him, tears welling in my eyes. "You really did it? You forged my signature so you could take the rest of the money Mom set aside for my college education when I have tuition due in less than a month?"

"Don't you dare bring your mother into this." He shook me to emphasize his point.

"We're gonna go down to the bank so you can get me that money, and I don't want any more backtalk from you."

Before I even had the chance to think about saying something else, he shoved me.

The sting of betrayal was almost worse than the actual physical pain. As awful as my dad had been since my mom's death, he'd never hurt me. But my arm would have fingertip-shaped bruises tomorrow, and there was a sharp sting in my ribs from how I landed wrong against the arm of the couch, which had almost no padding left.

Tears spilled down my cheeks, but he didn't react to them. Gulping down the lump in my throat, I whispered, "It's too late to go in now. They'll be closed by the time we get there."

"Fine," he huffed. "We'll go in the morning. Now get off your ass and make me some dinner."

I did as he asked, not bothering to eat anything since I was too upset to be hungry. Instead, I went up to my room and cried myself to sleep. Which was probably a good thing since I spent most of the night tossing and turning, unable to find a comfortable position as my mind kept replaying the confrontation with my dad over and over again. I didn't understand how he could have changed so much in such little time.

I felt so alone. With my mom gone and no family in the area, I didn't have anyone to turn to for advice. My friends from high school were spending their first summer break after college partying, and I hadn't talked to any of them about my problems with my dad because I felt as though I'd already leaned on them too much when my mom died.

By the time the next morning rolled around, I was tired and sore. And I hadn't come up with a way to stop my dad from destroying my future for his own selfish reasons, whatever they were.

The next few hours passed painfully slowly as I hid in my room and waited for him to sleep off all the beer he'd most likely drunk last night. Another big change from the man who'd barely finish one can when I was growing up.

I wasn't surprised that he still smelled like a brewery when he finally came into my room a little before noon. "Get your ass outta bed. We need to go to the bank. Now."

Climbing off my mattress, I dressed, then

grabbed a thin cardigan from my closet and pulled it on. The sleeves were short, but they were just long enough to hide the bruises on my arm. The last thing I needed was for someone at the bank to ask awkward questions while I filled out the paperwork that would give my dad access to my college savings.

When I got downstairs, he was already waiting at the door for me. "Hurry up, Tessa."

"I'm almost ready to go, but I don't—"

"You don't, what? Want to give me back my hard-earned dollars when it'll save my life?"

"Your life?" I echoed, glancing down at my bare feet. All I'd planned to say was that I just needed to put on a pair of sandals.

"I'm still not sure how it happened. I never would've put so much on the line in that poker game if I hadn't been up by a fuck ton." He raked his fingers through his hair. "But then I was on a losing streak, and before I knew what happened, I was in too deep. Now because some asshole had better luck than me, I need to come up with sixty thousand dollars before my bookie takes it outta my hide."

My dad had a bookie. And he owed the guy the equivalent of three years of my college education. All from one poker game, if my dad's irate muttering was to be believed.

I was still trying to wrap my head around the bombshell of information he'd just dropped when he yanked the door open and stomped outside, yelling at me to hurry up again. I didn't feel as though I had any other choice, so I slipped on my sandals and grabbed my purse. Then I headed off to the bank with my dad...to destroy my future.

The old saying about what you didn't know couldn't hurt you wasn't true in this situation. I had no clue that my dad had a gambling problem, but I was the one who would pay the price for his mistake.

2

PHANTOM

"I don't take checks," the florist snapped as she guarded the door to her delivery van.

Rom growled, and I grabbed his arm, holding him back. "Calm the fuck down, brother. You think not having flowers will upset your bride? How 'bout if her groom is in jail?"

"Jail?" the young, pinched-faced florist squeaked.

I shot her a warning glance. "Relax. No one is going to do shit to you. I'll run to the bank and get cash." I pointed my finger at the uptight woman who had shown up to deliver the wedding flowers. "But you better unload and get everything set up, or that might change when I return."

She narrowed her eyes at me, but then they went wide when she glanced to my side. I followed her gaze, seeing my prez, VP, and a few other brothers in the Silver Saints MC standing beside us. "Um... okay...just be sure to bring—"

"Yeah, yeah," I cut her off, already stomping to my bike parked a few feet away. "Just get your bony ass to work."

I didn't hear if she responded over the roar of my motorcycle engine starting, and I didn't give a fuck. With a chin lift from Mac, the president of my MC, letting him know I'd handle things from here, I pulled out and headed into town.

I was already irritated from coming to Layla's rescue when her overbearing mother wouldn't stop driving her crazy. I'd stepped in and practically dragged her to her seat where her husband waited and ordered him to keep her ass there.

Every patch in my MC was like a brother to me, and that made their old ladies like sisters, so we were all invested in what made the women happy. But I'd always been closest with Rom, and Layla had wormed her way into my heart, becoming the annoying little sister I never had and never wanted. But I'd be damned if some uptight florist ruined her wedding.

There was a short line at the bank, so it didn't take me long to withdraw the money. I stashed it in the inner pocket of my suit coat—I still had no idea how Rom talked us all into the monkey suits—and strode purposely toward the revolving door.

A woman dashed into one of the compartments, and I quickly slipped into the one behind her as she pushed frantically to get the glass moving. I was in a hurry too, but it didn't stop me from noticing that she had a spectacular ass for someone so small. Her jeans molded to the perfectly rounded globes, and her long auburn hair fell to just above them.

When fresh air hit me in the face, it broke my focus on the woman. I shook myself, surprised at how my body had reacted to just the back of some chick's body. Especially when my dick had basically taken a leave of absence a long time ago. Casual sex had never been my thing, and I'd joined the CIA when I graduated from college at twenty-one. Being a spook wasn't exactly conducive to relationships, then when I left The Company almost two years ago, I hadn't found a woman who'd interested me. Yet this stranger—*the back of her, for shit's sake*—had made my cock stir.

I shook my head, then grunted when I walked into something soft standing in my way.

I glanced down just as the woman hissed and bent over. Her breathing was suddenly labored and recognizing the sound—having caused it often enough during my years as an operative—concern had me rapidly moving so I was facing her.

She was still bent over, her arms wrapped around her torso, and her beautiful face contorted with pain.

"Sorry, sweetheart," I rasped, trying to focus despite being awestruck by how fucking gorgeous she was. "Are you okay?"

From what I saw, she had at least one broken rib and probably a few bruised ones.

"Yes. I'm sorry," she wheezed, although her breathing wasn't as shallow. and color was returning to her pale face. "I didn't mean to stop so fast. I was looking for..."

Her musical voice trailed off as she straightened, and her gaze traveled up my body, her head falling back so she could look at my face since I practically towered over her.

She doubled-blinked her jade-green eyes, and her mouth parted slightly, conjuring images of her puffy pink lips around my cock. I pushed them away and smiled at her dazed expression, then frowned when she sucked in a breath before wincing.

"What's wrong?" I asked. My tone was gruffer than I'd intended, but I was already picturing my hands around the throat of whoever had hurt my girl. *My girl?*

Well, shit. My brothers had been right. The second I looked in her eyes, I knew she was mine. The petite redhead with big tits and wide, round hips was obviously very young—too young for me. I guessed she was at least eighteen, although until I knew for sure, I shouldn't have been contemplating how to get her under me. But the truth was, it didn't matter to me. I was going to claim her anyway, even if I had to wait to do it.

When she shook her head and backed up, I worried that my tone and angry expression might be scaring her. But I didn't see any fear when I locked eyes with her. There was confusion, but I was also satisfied by the desire simmering in them.

When she took one more step, her foot got caught on the seam in the sidewalk, and she began to stumble backward. My hands shot out, and I gently clutched her biceps, but I immediately shifted my hold to her shoulders when she whimpered and grimaced.

"What the fuck?" I muttered. I dropped one hand to her wrist and used the other to shove up the sleeve of her sweater. Bruises in the shape of fingertips marred her perfect skin, and I growled as rage built up inside me.

"Tessa! Let's go." My head whipped up to see a man who resembled my girl with the same green eyes and auburn hair. He stomped over to her, clearly not even noticing me as he scowled at her and grabbed her other arm, gripping it tight. "Stupid fucking bank," he muttered as he forced her to go with him in the opposite direction.

I was about to go after her when my phone rang, and I remembered why I'd come to town. *Fucking hell.* I needed to go after her. But I also couldn't disappoint Rom and Layla by skipping out on their wedding...especially when I was a groomsman.

In the end, I decided to get back to the wedding, despite my heart screaming at me, demanding I go find her. However, if I hopped on my bike and followed them, there was a good chance that the man —who I assumed was her father—would call the cops and I'd be detained, screwing over all of my intentions. After so many years of being a spy, I knew how to be invisible, but there was no way to hide while riding a motorcycle...especially my hog.

The logical thing to do was call Grey or Hack, two brothers who were world class hackers. They could locate her, and I'd go get her as soon as they did.

Pissed as fuck at the shitty situation, I stalked to my bike, slammed my helmet on my head, and took off like a bat outta hell.

Once I arrived back at the church, I shoved the money at the florist, then stomped through the building until I found Grey. He sat with his old lady in one of the church pews, but he took one look at my face and kissed her cheek, then murmured something and stood. I pivoted and stalked to an empty corner at the back of the chapel, grabbing a tithing envelope and a pen on the way.

"What's up?" Grey asked in a low voice so we wouldn't be overheard.

"Need you to track someone down," I muttered as I began writing everything I could remember about Tessa and our encounter on the little envelope.

Music began playing, and I silently cursed, knowing I needed to take my place because the wedding was about to start. I finished scribbling my notes and shoved it at Grey. "It's not much to go on, but this is top fucking priority, brother."

Grey skimmed it and shrugged. "I've worked with less." He peered at me and cocked his head. "Mac approve this as top priority?"

Frustrated, I grunted and shook my head. "Haven't had a chance to tell him, but...she's mine."

He absorbed my words for a minute, then our attention shifted to the large, carved wood chapel doors as they were propped open, and ushers escorted the first guests to their seats. Grey slipped the paper into his pocket and lifted his chin toward the dais at the front of the room. "I'll get on this as soon as we get back to the hotel tonight. We better get to our places."

I nodded and made my way up to the front. Rom was pacing under the flower arch, and I rolled my eyes as I approached him. "Worried she's gonna ditch your grumpy ass?" Rom glared at me but cracked a smile when I laughed and grabbed his hand to pull him in for a back-slapping hug. "Happy for you, brother," I told him before taking my place with the other groomsmen.

The ceremony was probably very nice, but as hard as I tried, I couldn't pay attention. All I could think about was Tessa and what she might be going through at that moment. The only thing that kept me sane was the glimpse of irritation I'd seen on her face —rather than terror—when her father had pulled her away. I'd instinctively known she had some fire in her, but I was willing to bet that she was going along with whatever predicament she was in to keep the peace while she figured things out. Well, I was about to sort that shit out for her.

I saw through as much of the reception as I could, but when I spotted Rom and Mac waiting for their women by the restroom, I stormed over to where they lounged against the wall.

"Mac."

They both looked up, and their brows furrowed at my furious expression and tone. "I need help," I growled.

Mac frowned and pushed off the wall. "Whatever you need, Phantom. What's goin' on?"

"I saw...I met...fuck!" I cursed as I ran my hands over my head. "My woman. I found her. But...there were bruises. Shit. I have to get to her."

"We'll handle it," Mac assured me, giving me a small trickle of relief. Not that I had expected Mac to brush off my request. Whether Tessa had been my woman or not, if I'd told him that I met an abused woman who needed our help, he would have been just as ready to help.

"You talk to Grey or Hack already?" he inquired.

I nodded. "Grey'll start searching as soon as they get back to the hotel tonight. I'm headed back now so that I'm ready when he finds out anything."

Mac nodded but didn't say anything since his old lady, Bridget, and Rom's bride, Layla, stepped out of the bathroom. He kissed his woman's forehead and smacked her ass. "I'll meet you by the cake, baby."

Bridget looked around at the three of us, then patted me on the shoulder as she passed. "Your turn, huh?"

Layla looked at Rom with a question in her eyes, but he shook his head and took her hand. Then he glanced at me and Mac. "Let me know if I'm needed," he said before walking away with his bride.

"You know who's hurting her?" Mac questioned.

"Pretty sure it's her father," I snarled, feeling even more angered that she was suffering at the hands of someone whose job it was to protect her.

"Fuck," he muttered.

"Something about the way he looked at her, almost desperate. And the irritation in her expression when he dragged her away. I think there's more to the story. I need to get her away from him."

"No question," he agreed. "But if it's her parent..." He stared at the wall for a moment and stroked his beard. When he met my eyes again, I knew what he was about to ask.

"I don't know how old she is. If I had to guess, I'd

say over eighteen, but I won't know for sure until Grey tracks her down."

Mac sighed and crossed his lean arms over his broad chest. "You know we'll handle this either way," he assured me. "But it'll be a fuck of a lot harder if she isn't legal, especially if the abuser is a parent."

"Understood." I'd already thought through many, many scenarios. "One more thing."

Mac raised a silver eyebrow and waited.

"She's injured. Patch is headed home in the morning, and even if he wasn't, he doesn't have a clinic here..." I trailed off, knowing he would pick up on my request without my needing to voice it.

"You want me to put in a call to Fox." It was a statement, not a question, so I didn't respond.

Patch was our club doctor. He had a clinic attached to our clubhouse, but we were in Old Bridge, where Layla was from—a couple of hours from the Silver Saints compound.

Through Grey's old lady, we had a connection to the VP of the local MC, the Iron Rogues. The prez, Fox, ran their club in the same way Mac handled the Silver Saints. Their activities weren't exactly legal, but they weren't involved in dirty shit like drugs or the sex trade. They respected women and were known to help people who needed to disappear. But most importantly, they had their own doctor.

"I'll give him a call and let you know what he says. Go on back to the hotel so you're ready when Grey has her location."

I jerked my chin up in acknowledgment, then turned and headed to the parking lot.

3
___
TESSA

Glancing down at my cell phone as it rang, I saw the name of one of my high school friends flash across the screen. I wasn't in the mood to talk to anyone, but that didn't stop me from answering. At the very least, connecting with Sarah was a temporary reprieve from the bone-deep loneliness I was feeling.

"Hello."

"Hey, girl. I feel like it's been forever since we've seen each other."

Flopping against my mattress, I stared up at my ceiling. "Yeah, it does."

"That's why you need to come to the lake with us today," she suggested. "Brian's dad said he could take the boat out, so you know it's gonna be a blast."

So much for Sarah providing a happy distraction. Her invitation only made me feel worse because the last time I went out on the lake with my friends was the day before my mom's fatal car accident. She'd packed a cooler full of food and sent me on my way with a smile. It was the last time I'd seen her, and the reminder of that day plummeted my bad mood even further.

The invitation also drove home why I couldn't turn to my old friends for help—their lives were centered around themselves. If Sarah had really wanted to see me, she would've suggested anything other than a day on the lake. A good friend would've stopped to think about how much the reminder of my mom would hurt me.

Barely holding back tears, I mumbled, "Thanks, but I can't make it. Sorry, maybe next time."

Not giving Sarah the chance to reply, I ended the call and buried my face in my pillow. Just when I thought my day couldn't get any worse, I had to be reminded again of what I'd lost when my mom died.

Any hope that I had of getting my old dad back disappeared when I handed the completed paperwork over to the bank employee yesterday. He hadn't cared that he'd gambled my future away. All he'd wanted was the money my mom had scrimped and saved to give me the education she'd always wanted.

I had no idea how I would pay for my college next semester, but I needed to figure something out so I wasn't stuck living with my dad for any longer than I needed to. Even if I had to drop out of school and get a job to pay for rent, I wanted to get away from here before the end of summer.

Rolling over, I grabbed the framed picture of my mom that I kept on my bedside table. Sniffling to hold back my tears, I whispered, "I really wish you were still here, Mom. Miss you so much."

My dad rapped his knuckles against my door, and I hugged the photo to my chest as he popped his head inside my bedroom. "Get up and make me breakfast."

As I listened to him stomp down the stairs, I pressed a kiss to my mom's face before setting the picture back down. Then I did what I'd done every morning since I'd come home from college for the summer—cooked my dad over easy eggs, sausage links, and toast.

I'd been hurt that he barely spoke to me other than to make demands. Make food. Clean the house. Do the laundry. My father had treated me as the hired help instead of his daughter, but that was nothing new since he'd basically done the same last summer before I left for school. And after what happened yesterday, I was relieved that he didn't pay attention to me while eating.

When he was done, he pushed the empty plate toward the middle of the table. Leaving it there, he stood and grabbed his keys off the hook by the door that led to the garage. "I'm headed out to run some errands. Won't be gone too long."

I hoped like heck "errands" wasn't code for another poker game before the bank had even processed my withdrawal request. "Okay."

I didn't understand why he bothered to tell me what he was doing until he added, "Log into your bank account and see if they did anything with the paperwork yet."

"Will do," I muttered, gritting my teeth so hard, I was surprised they didn't crumble under the pressure.

He hadn't been happy to learn that the person who handled college savings accounts wasn't in the office on Saturdays. He'd wanted that money right away, but I'd been told the earliest the check would be cut was Monday morning. That didn't stop him from asking me to check the account last night. Or again today, apparently.

As soon as I heard his car pull out of the garage, I made myself a bowl of cereal. While I munched away, I searched online for job opportunities in my college town. I figured the best-case scenario was that I found a way to pay for the upcoming semester since I already had my dorm room lined up for the year. Qualifying for an apartment when you were nineteen with no job or credit history was nearly impossible from what I'd found online earlier this morning.

Unfortunately, so was coming up with a way to pay for college since I wasn't having much luck at locating any scholarships that still had open applications. And qualifying for any grants required my dad to fill out his part of the financial aid application, which I didn't see happening. Loans were probably my only option at this point, but I needed his help with getting those too.

Considering I was in this position because he had a gambling problem, that seemed like a big risk. If my dad knew how easy they were to get, there was a chance he'd saddle me with more than I could ever pay back...and I'd still be in the same position because he'd run out and blow it on another poker game.

I needed help, and I couldn't stop thinking about

the big guy I'd bumped into as I was walking out of the bank yesterday. Although he'd been dressed nicely in a gray suit that didn't do a thing to hide how muscular he was, there was still a dangerous air to him. Which was why it was ridiculous that I kept picturing him as the hero who would come riding to my rescue. Then again, with his intense blue eyes, short, dark hair, and the five o'clock shadow on his chiseled jaw, it wasn't a surprise that I couldn't get him off my mind. Especially with how tall he was and the muscles that were impossible to miss when I'd crashed into him.

But it wasn't as if he would miraculously show up on my doorstep to solve all of my problems since we were strangers. Although, he looked like a man who knew how to get stuff done. And the extra years he had on me—at least fifteen if I had to guess—meant he had way more experience than I did with figuring stuff out. Which was probably why my brain had fixated on him as my only way out of this mess. That and the fact that he was the first man who'd ever made my panties wet...and that was saying a lot, considering the circumstances.

A hard knock on the front door pulled me out of my thoughts, and I set my laptop down on the coffee table before padding over to see who it was. It was a good thing I wasn't a gambler like my dad because if I'd placed a bet on who it was, I would've lost.

Almost as if I'd conjured him out of thin air, the man from the sidewalk stood in front of me. "It's you."

"Damn straight it's me."

He gripped my waist to nudge me back into the house, kicking the door shut behind us. I should've been scared by the big stranger who'd basically just forced his way into my home, but he'd been so gentle with me when he'd done it. And there was a tender gleam in his eyes that tugged at my heartstrings. "I don't understand."

"I couldn't leave town knowing that I left you behind with bruises on your pretty skin." He wrapped his fingers around my wrist and carefully turned my arm. Fury filled his blue orbs as he stared down at the marks my father's fingers had left behind. "Need to know who I'm gonna end for hurting you."

His eyes flicked to a family portrait on the wall, and I briefly wondered if he knew it was my dad.

Was he serious? Whoa. He really was my knight in shining armor.

4

PHANTOM

I'd been across the street from her house in a motel parking lot for nearly four hours. Ever since Grey had tracked down her location—which had taken far too fucking long. Fifteen years with The Company had taught me how to be inconspicuous. I'd been waiting for her father to leave before approaching, knowing it would be a fuck of a lot easier to get her away.

But looking at her bruises, part of me wished he was still around so I could give him a taste of his own medicine. I didn't want my woman witnessing that kind of brutality.

That might send her running and screaming in the opposite direction, though. So it was for the best that we were alone.

"Um, kill?" she asked in a breathless voice.

I wasn't sure if it was fear or excitement, and that intrigued me. I doubted she was a bloodthirsty little thing, so I hoped it was more of that fire I'd glimpsed inside her.

My brain told me to tread lightly and not let on how absolutely obsessed I already was with her, but my hands had a mind of their own, and they cupped her cheeks. "I would do anything to protect you, sweet girl."

Her eyes widened with surprise, but a glimmer of hope emanated from their depths. Maybe I should have expected her reaction because she'd been made just for me.

"Now, tell me who hurt you."

"I...I don't even know your name," she whispered, making no move to free herself from my hands.

I closed my eyes and shook my head, exasperated with myself and more than grateful that she was taking this all in stride. "Sorry. I'm Phantom." For some reason, that didn't sit right. "Actually, my name is Kian. You call me Kian," I corrected myself.

"Phantom?"

I smirked. "It's my road name, sweet girl," I

explained, then released her to twist, showing off the back of my cut. "But like I said, you call me Kian."

"Okay," she agreed, making me smile.

When I turned back around, she was studying me curiously. "The Silver Saints? You're in a motorcycle club?"

"Yeah."

"Like in the movies?" She actually looked eager for me to confirm her assumption, which I found adorable as fuck.

But I rolled my eyes and took her hand, leading her over to a couch in the small living room to our right. "The movies are shit," I told her as I gently pushed on her shoulders to sit, then I took the cushion right next to her. "Don't get me wrong, there are some fucked-up clubs out there, ones similar to what Hollywood portrays"—I chuckled, thinking about some of the old ladies in the club—"and those smutty books chicks read."

Tessa's cheeks bloomed with pink, and a devilish smile spread across my face. From what my brothers had told me, the stories were garbage, but they had some excellent ideas to try out in bed. And other places.

"Um, so...anyway...I guess I should tell you my name is Tessa."

"I know."

She frowned, her face clouding with confusion. "How do you know...wait. How did you even find me?"

"Connections. I'll explain another time. Right now, I need you to answer my question. Whose motherfucking fingerprints are those?" I gestured to her arm.

Her eyelids descended as she dropped her gaze to the ground, hiding her beautiful green gems. I lifted her face with my index finger under her chin. "I'm going to protect you, sweet girl. No one will ever hurt you again."

She bit her lip and studied me, contemplating my words until she finally made up her mind and spoke. "My father. He didn't really mean to, sort of. He just...he was mad and being careless and..."

"He didn't mean to break his daughter's fucking ribs?" I growled.

Tessa cringed. "Well, he was upset and shoved me, and I fell against the couch." She grabbed my arm when I shot to my feet, ready to hunt the motherfucker down and break every one of his bones. "I'm not making excuses for him. What he did to me was wrong. Everything he has done. But it's hard for me to think that the loving father I once had has disappeared completely. He hadn't physically abused me before yesterday, and it wasn't on purpose...he was only focused on himself. I don't think he really even processed that he'd hurt me. He's acting out of desperation."

That got my attention, dragging up the memory of his expression when he dragged her away from the bank. "Explain," I demanded as I sat back down.

Tessa sighed and told me about her mom's death and the change it had brought in her father. "Growing up, he was everything a dad should be. Loving, happy, and I was his little princess." Moisture gathered in her eyes, and I used my thumb to wipe one away when it escaped. Her tears gutted me.

"During the days right after her death, he started to pull away. Soon after her funeral, he barely spoke to me anymore. He was gone all the time, and when he was home, he was in a bad mood. I—" She stopped, and her face flushed as her gaze dropped to her lap.

"You can tell me anything, sweet girl," I urged her. Then I admitted, "Nothing you say will come close to the shit I've done. Don't be embarrassed."

"I was so relieved to leave for college," she said,

her shoulders drooping. "Maybe if I'd stuck around, I could have helped him—"

"Don't," I grunted. "This isn't on you, Tessa. That motherfucker is a grown ass man whose daughter needed him. Don't go blaming yourself for shit that's outta your control."

Maybe I should have felt an iota of sympathy for the man losing his wife. However, there was no compassion in me because he'd been so selfishly absorbed by his own grief that he'd not only neglected his daughter but treated her like a pawn to feed his addiction.

"Anyway," she continued after giving me a soft smile. "I found out recently that he has a gambling problem. He owes his bookie a lot of money. That's why he was so upset. He tried to empty my college fund, but the bank called me for permission. I had to be the one to withdraw it, and he was angry when I confronted him."

"That's what you were doing at the bank?"

She nodded. "But they can't cut the check for a couple of days."

I made a mental note to get the information for her account and give it to Grey. "I know someone who can figure something out so your dad can't get his hands on your money and you can finish school."

Tessa's gaze swung over to the fireplace where a large family portrait hung over it. "I don't really care about school, to be honest. My first year there was fine, I guess. But it mostly was a means of getting away from my dad. I have nowhere else to go, and without that money, I'm stuck here."

"Not anymore," I grunted as I pushed to my feet. "You're coming with me."

She shook her head, then dropped it back so she could look up at my face with an expression of wonder. "I don't even know your last name. But for some reason, I feel safe with you."

I smiled and bent down to clasp her hands and pull her up. "You have good instincts," I told her. Instead of saying what I really wanted to—that she was mine. I'd thrown enough at her, I didn't want to push my luck. "Go pack a bag, baby."

"Where are we going?"

I turned her toward a staircase across the hall and patted her ass to get her moving. "Right now, I'm taking you somewhere to have your injuries checked out."

"A hospital?" Her face screwed up like she smelled something bad. "I don't like them."

"Good thing I know someone who does house calls," I teased.

"Then why aren't they coming here?"

I sighed and walked her over to the bottom of the stairs. "It was more like a figure of speech, baby. Now go get some shit so we can go see a doctor. No hospital, I promise."

She came back down with a small duffel less than five minutes later. I took the bag, then put my hand on her back and guided her out the front door. We walked to the driveway, and she halted. "Where is your car?" she asked as her gaze swept the empty driveway and the curb in front of the house.

"No car," I murmured, pressing on her back to get her moving again. It was the wrong time for a confrontation with her dad, and I'd already tested chance by staying at her house for so long since I had no idea where he'd gone.

"What?" She stopped again and looked up at me like I was crazy. "How are we leaving?"

"Motorcycle club," I said, patting my cut. "What do you think I rode here?"

"B-but–I–um–I've never ridden a motorcycle!" she sputtered.

I grinned. "Good. I'm your first."

Tessa turned beet red, and I wanted to beat my chest like a caveman because I knew she was thinking about a different first. My girl was a virgin.

It wouldn't have changed a damn thing about what I felt for her if she hadn't been. But knowing I would pop her cherry, that I was the only one who would ever feel her sweet pussy wrapped around me, and the only one to see what she looked like in the throes of ecstasy...it was intoxicating and made it hard as fuck—literally—not to grab a room in that motel and make her mine right then and there.

However, I didn't want my first time with my woman to be rushed or in a crappy motel. So I used the walk across the street to calm my raging hormones and talk my dick into standing down.

I managed to get myself to a point where the ride wouldn't be excruciating. Well, that was what I thought until I was riding down the road with my woman's soft body pressed against me, her arms gripping my torso, and the heat between her legs radiating through both layers of our clothing.

Fuck. Fuck. Fuck.

Taking things slow with Tessa just might kill me.

5

TESSA

When I fantasized about Kian riding in to save me, I hadn't imagined that it would be on a motorcycle. Being on the back of it with him was amazing. I loved the freedom I felt as the wind whipped around us...and being wrapped around his muscular body. But pulling up in front of a motorcycle club was still one heck of a surprise.

When Kian parked in front of a sprawling concrete building—after driving through a manned gate, for goodness' sake—I asked, "I thought you said you were taking me to someone who does house calls?"

"The Iron Rogues have a doctor who's a member, like we do," he explained as he climbed off the bike and then helped me to my feet. "I'd prefer that you saw Patch for your injury, but that's not an option. So Blade will have to do."

"Thanks for the ringing endorsement."

Kian grinned at the big guy standing in the doorway. "You can't blame me for preferring Patch when he's my club brother and I've seen him work."

"From what Mac told my prez when he called, you're stuck with me today unless you want to go to the hospital. Which you're still welcome to do, even though I'm a fuck of a lot better than the doctor you'd end up with in the emergency room. Not to mention you won't have to wait for fucking ever to be seen." His gaze landed on me, and he asked, "She's my patient?"

Kian stepped between us. "Yeah, but give us a second."

"Sure, Phantom. No rush. It's not as though you dragged my ass to the clubhouse so I could help you out as a favor between our presidents or anything like that," the other man muttered as he walked back inside.

When the door closed behind him, Kian turned to me. Gaping up at him, I whispered, "That's the doctor who's going to take a look at my ribs?"

"Yup, but don't worry," he reassured me as he started to slip his leather vest off his shoulders. "I know he looks a little rough around the edges, but he's still a damn good doctor. The shit I give him for not being Patch is all about club loyalty and nothing to do with his ability to treat you. I never would've brought you here if I didn't think he'd do a good job. I'd never risk you like that."

After everything my dad had put me through since my mom died, the way Kian was looking out for me was almost more than I could bear...but in the best way possible. Sniffling so I didn't cry, I murmured, "Thank you."

"I know that you don't know me well enough yet to get this, but you can always count on me to have your back, sweet girl," he vowed, sincerity shining from his blue orbs.

"I'm starting to see that."

"Good." He slid his vest onto my shoulders and tugged my arms through the holes. "One of the ways I'm gonna protect you today is to have you wear my cut, so everyone in there will know you're with me."

With our size difference, the vest went all the way down to my mid-thigh. "Umm...is this really necessary? Won't they already know if you're right there with me?"

"I'm gonna stick by your side while we're in there but putting you in my cut sends a stronger statement." Placing his palm against my lower back, he guided me toward the door. "It's a biker thing."

"I guess I'll have to trust you on that since I know nothing about motorcycle clubs."

"No worries, plenty of the Silver Saint old ladies had no clue what MCs were about when they met their men, but they all adjusted just fine." Kian shook his head with a deep chuckle. "Which was probably for the best now that I think about it, since our club is a fuck of a lot different from others. Especially when it comes to how we treat women."

I blinked my eyes to adjust to the dim lighting, my head turning in the direction of the masculine voice that said, "Only because you guys have all taken the whole love-at-first-sight thing way too far. Dropping like flies left and right ever since your prez found his old lady."

"We also don't go around kidnapping innocent women just because their brother had the nerve to hook up with one of our sisters," Kian muttered, pulling me against his side. "But you can't say the same, can you, Maverick?"

"Maybe not," Maverick conceded, looking only slightly sheepish as he shrugged. "But no Iron Rogue has kidnapped the woman he loves. You can't say the same about the Silver Saints, can you, Phantom?"

Kidnapping? My eyes widened, and my head jerked back so I could gawk up at Kian.

"Don't worry, sweet girl. It's not as bad as it sounds." Kian gave me a comforting squeeze. "My club brothers would readily lay down their lives to keep their women safe."

"Shit, sorry." Maverick raked his fingers through his hair. "I didn't mean to scare your girl."

"Quit pushing each other's buttons. The beef between our clubs has been settled," Blade grumbled, jerking his chin toward a hallway to our left. "Come on back to my clinic before you two start something else. I don't want to call Fox and ask him to join us down here because you couldn't keep your mouths shut."

Maverick crossed his arms over his broad chest and quirked a brow. "Our prez knew damn well how I run my mouth when he picked me to be his second in charge. The man has known me my entire life."

"Whatever, man." Blade shook his head as he strode toward the hallway, pausing to look over his shoulder at Kian and me. "You coming?"

"Yup," Kian confirmed, guiding me to follow the other man.

I had serious doubts about the situation I'd found myself in, but the warmth of Kian's palm against my back offered a comfort I hadn't felt in so long. And when Blade waved us into a large room that had more medical equipment than most urgent cares, more of my concern melted away.

Kian helped me onto the nearest exam table, and I flashed him a shy smile. "Thanks."

"Like I said," he moved to stand at my side, "I've got your back. Always."

I nodded, interlacing my fingers through his when he reached for my hand. "Okay."

"I get that you're nervous, but no harm will come to you while you're here." Blade moved to my other side and looked across the exam table at Kian. "And judging by the fact that you're wearing Phantom's cut, you don't have to worry about anyone messing with you when you leave, either. He wasn't exaggerating when he said that the Silver Saints would die before they let one of their old ladies get hurt. Whoever hurt you doesn't stand a chance against him."

I ducked my head, my cheeks heating. It had been embarrassing enough to admit to Kian that my father was the one who'd hurt me. I didn't want to explain what happened to anyone else.

Squeezing my hand, Kian growled, "Tessa knows she's safe with me. What we don't know is if her ribs are broken. That's what we came to you for."

"Then I guess that's what I'd better do." He grabbed a stethoscope from a nearby counter. "Gonna need you to lift your shirt so I can see the damage."

"Sure." The pink in my cheeks deepened as I followed his directions.

I caught my breath when he prodded my side with his fingers, muttering, "The swelling isn't bad, but it bruised like a motherfucker. You were hurt yesterday?"

"Yeah."

"Take a deep breath." I winced as I sucked in air, and he asked, "How bad is the pain when you do that?"

"A little worse, but not as bad as I expected."

"That's a good sign that it might not be broken."

Kian shifted closer to me, and Blade shot him a look. "Relax, Phantom. I wasn't going to assume she's okay. I'm going to do an x-ray to make sure."

"Okay."

"Unless you're pregnant?" He shot a look at Kian. "If I didn't know it was scientifically impossible, I'd say there's something in the water over at the Silver Saints compound."

"Um, no. We just met yesterday," I whispered.

"Quit embarrassing my sweet girl and get this shit done," Kian directed.

Sighing over how he used his cute nickname for me, I followed Blade over to the x-ray machine. I was a little worried by how at ease he was with getting the images he needed because it made me wonder how often one of the Iron Rogues got seriously injured. But it was nice not having to wait for the results.

I was so relieved when he said, "I have good news. No fractures, just deep bruising. You're gonna need to protect that side, rotate between ice and heat for ten to twenty minutes at a time, and take over-the-counter pain meds as needed. Let Patch know if you don't see improvement with the pain or it gets worse."

"Thank you so much," I murmured as I fixed my shirt and let Kian's leather vest settle around my body.

"Is she healthy enough to handle being on the back of my bike for two hours?" Kian asked.

"Yup, as long as Tessa pays attention to what her body tells her, she's good to go," Blade confirmed. "If the ribs start to bother her, pull off the road for a little bit to give her a break."

6

PHANTOM

Before leaving the Iron Rogues compound, I put Tessa on the phone with Grey and had her answer all of his questions so he could work on keeping her money out of her dad's hands now that I'd gotten her away from him.

Once she was done, I stowed my phone in one of my saddle bags and put my helmet on her head. The corners of my mouth curved up because she looked so damn cute. I'd have to get her one of her own as soon as possible.

"Where are we going now?" she asked softly. "And why did you ask Blade if I could handle a two-hour ride? It sounds like fun, but I need to figure out what I'm going to do next because I'm scared to go back home."

Apparently, I hadn't been very clear about what was happening. "You're not going back to your dad's house, sweet girl. There is no fucking way I will ever let him harm you again."

She frowned, and her forehead creased with her confusion. "I have nowhere else to go, Kian. School doesn't start for—"

"You're coming with me," I informed her. "We can figure out school later. Right now, I just need you safe and with me." If she wanted to finish school, I had no problem with that, but she'd have to transfer to somewhere closer to home because she wasn't going to live anywhere but with me.

I was prepared to argue with her, but she looked up at me through her long auburn lashes, and her plump lips curved into a small smile. "Okay."

Pleased with her response, I returned her smile and gave her waist a gentle squeeze before lifting her onto my bike. Since she was so tiny, I was grateful that I'd added higher foot pegs so I could take some of the older kids on rides. Our motorcycles were practically sacred, so other than a few of my brothers' tween spawn, Tessa would be the first female to ever ride on mine. It had always bothered me to think of a woman taking up space while I was riding, but I'd loved every second of the ride to the Iron

Rogues' doc, other than the painful situation in my jeans.

"I don't have much with me," Tessa reminded me with a worried expression. "My stuff..."

"We'll get all your shit later, baby. We'll figure out the rest when we get home."

Once we were both situated, we hit the road. Tessa was a natural. She held me firmly, but the longer we rode, the more I felt the tension ease out of her. Although, I was sure that some of that was also due to the distance we were putting between her and her father.

He'd never be able to get to her on the SS compound, which was the only reason I was glad to be taking her there. After spending so many years as a spy, a lot of people preferred solitude. But for me, I had enough of the loneliness, so when I retired, I moved into the clubhouse.

I'd kept my shit there anyway because I was rarely home, so why pay for an apartment? However, as we neared home, it was the first time I wished I had a place of my own. Somewhere Tessa and I could truly be alone. Although, until we knew the extent of her situation—including whether her dad's bookie would come after her when he didn't get his money—she was safest at the clubhouse.

But I'd start looking for places for Tessa to choose from immediately. After moving up in the ranks and having very little expenses for the past seventeen years, I'd built up a hefty nest egg, so we didn't need her money to live very comfortably.

It was midafternoon when I parked my bike in the lot by the entrance to Silver Ink, a tattoo parlor—one of the many businesses owned by the club—on the compound, along with our garage, Silver Auto and Restoration. These were the only two buildings on the property that could be accessed by people who weren't members, old ladies, or invited guests. The customers used a separate public entrance, but right next to them, inside the compound, was a parking lot for motorcycles.

I helped Tessa down and stowed my helmet before taking her hand and leading her around the corner to the main entrance of the clubhouse. The driveway, and a smaller lot on the other side, were where we generally parked any other vehicles.

Considering the packed state of both lots, something was clearly going on, but I couldn't remember anything being planned. Then again, my mind had basically emptied of everything that didn't have to do with my woman over the past two days.

"Fanta!"

I heard the name shouted as I opened the door and instantly dropped down, bracing myself as a blur of limbs and dark-blond hair barreled at me. "Hey, Opie," I grunted as the adorable two-year-old threw herself into my arms.

Opal was the daughter of our VP, Scout, and Cat, his old lady. I wasn't sure how it happened, but she'd had me wrapped around her tiny fingers since the moment the couple brought her to the clubhouse for the first time.

"Miss you," she said as she looked up at my face with a pout that would make every actress in Hollywood jealous.

"I missed you too, Opie."

"Stop calling my daughter Opie," Cat snapped as she exited the kitchen into the lounge. I grinned, and Scout, who was sitting on the couch drinking a beer, rolled his eyes.

"He does that just to piss you off, babe," he said to his wife as she dropped into his lap. "Why do you rise to the bait?"

Cat snatched his drink and took a long pull, then glared at me. "I don't want her to think that's her actual name just because her favorite person calls her that." When she referred to me as Opal's "favorite person," Cat's pout rivaled her toddler's.

"I let her call me the name of a soda brand," I argued…because picking at her was so much fun. Cat was cool as a cucumber most of the time, the only exception was when it came to her kids or her man.

"Because she hasn't learned how to say Phantom, jackass," Cat muttered.

"Ack ass!" Opal screamed, making me burst into laughter. "Ass ass ass!"

"That's on you, kitty cat," Scout told her with a grin before tipping back his bottle and draining it.

"Says the man who taught our five-year-old son to say mudderfucker," Cat grumped.

That had been fucking hysterical. It had taken Scout and Cat a week to get Griffin to stop shouting it everywhere they went.

"Fuck!" Opal shouted, and Cat dropped her face into her hands while Scout and I roared with laughter.

"At least she removes the semi-permanent scowl from your face," Cat sighed, winking at me.

I grinned and kissed a wiggly Opal on the cheek, then let her run off to play.

"I have a feeling we'll be seeing a lot more of those smiles," Scout drawled as his eyes shifted to the woman at my side, lingering on her chest before meeting my eyes and raising one brow. A stranger might have assumed he was checking out my woman, but I knew his attention had been caught by the fact that Tessa was still wearing my cut.

I nodded, and he grinned before giving Cat a quick kiss and moving her off his lap. Then he stood and meandered toward the long bar that ran the length of one side of the room. "'Bout damn time," he muttered.

Cat's gaze quickly followed where Scout's had been, and she lit up like a Christmas tree...or something a little more evil. "You fell, huh?"

"What?" a female voice shrieked, and I cringed when I spotted Knight's old lady, Kiara, walking into the room, rubbing her very large stomach. "Phantom?" Her smile was also wicked. "Oh, this is going to be fun."

Yeah, they were gonna be a pain in my ass. But I kind of deserved it after giving my brothers shit for being pussy-whipped and swearing it would never happen to me.

I slipped my arm around Tessa's waist, careful of her ribs, and tucked her into my side. "This is Tessa," I introduced her. Then I pointed at each one and told my girl their names as well.

Bridget had come into the room with Mac by the

time I finished, but rather than just telling her their names, I walked her over to meet them.

"Tessa, this is the president of the MC, Mac, and his old lady, Bridget."

"Welcome," Bridget said warmly. "Don't worry, there is no test. You can ask us our names as many times as you need to." She winked, and Tessa giggled. The sound made warmth flood my chest, and I decided I wanted to hear that sweet laugh every day for the rest of my life.

"Grey able to do it?" I asked Mac.

He nodded. "He's got all the account info for you." Then he looked down at Tessa. "Welcome to the Silver Saints, Tessa. You need anything at all, you can come to me or Bridget. Especially if you need someone to kick Phantom's ass for any reason."

She giggled again, and I huffed. "Good luck with that, old man."

Mac stared at me stonily, and I finally shrugged, making a corner of his mouth twitch. Mac was in his mid-fifties, but he was still a tough, strong, deadly motherfucker. Even with all my training, and being over sixteen years his junior, if we went head-to-head, I honestly couldn't have told you who would win.

"Party out back," he grunted, then he smirked.

"Molly is watching the kids." Molly was their fifteen-year-old daughter and the oldest of their four kids. Grabbing his wife's hand, he yanked her to him and tossed her over his shoulder before heading toward the stairs that went up to the rooms. "See you...later."

"Mac!" Bridget gasped, her face turning bright red, but then she laughed the rest of the way up the stairs.

"It can get a little crazy here," I mumbled as I peeked down to see how Tessa was handling all of this.

She smiled brightly, soothing my worry. "It's always so quiet at home, and I tend to spend most of my time at school in my single dorm room, so this is...awesome."

"Come on out to the barbecue," Cat invited us, gesturing to the kitchen door since we had to go through it to get to the back door.

Tessa nodded when I gave her a questioning look, and I kissed her forehead before guiding her toward the party. As we walked past Cat, she winked at me and whispered, "I like her."

Tessa was easy to like, and the SS old ladies were all friendly and accepting, but I was still relieved that she had Bridget and Cat in her corner. Especially because those two were scary as fuck when they went into mama bear mode, and I knew they'd already taken Tessa under their wings.

Behind the clubhouse kitchen was about an acre of cleared land with all kinds of outdoor activities for the kids, rows of picnic tables, half a dozen grills, and a couple of areas with firepits and lounging furniture surrounding them.

The party was in full swing, filling the air with delicious smells, music, adult laughter, and children screaming in delight.

"This is amazing," Tessa breathed.

My heart thumped hard, and I fell for her just a little bit more.

My woman was perfect. Perfect for me.

7

TESSA

When Kian had told me that he was taking me home with him, I'd been an odd combination of relieved, excited, and more than a little nervous. The thought of going home and facing my dad was daunting, especially when one of the neighbors was bound to tell him that I'd gone roaring off on a motorcycle with a man. The opportunity to spend more time with Kian was thrilling because it gave me the chance to get to know the intriguing, sexy man better. But hanging out at an MC clubhouse was far outside my comfort zone since my only experience before now was our short stop at the Iron Rogues when Blade checked my ribs. And although the members I had met during our visit to their clubhouse were kind to me, I hadn't felt as though I belonged there.

I was surprised to find the same couldn't be said for what I experienced when we arrived at Kian's clubhouse. The atmosphere at the Silver Saints compound was so different from the Iron Rogues. There were wives and children running around, and everyone smiled and greeted me as though I was family. I experienced a sense of belonging that was unexpected but very welcome.

"Having a good time, sweet girl?"

I tilted my head back to smile up at Kian. "I really am."

"I'm glad." He jerked his chin toward the food-covered tables to our right. "Did you get enough to eat?"

"More than enough." I patted my belly with a laugh. "I don't think I could handle one more bite."

"I hope you're wrong because dessert is not to be missed at our barbecues." Placing his palm on my lower back, he guided me over to a table loaded down with cookies, pies, and cake. "I could happily devour one of Cat's pies all by myself, but I'd have a battle on my hands with my club brothers if I took more than one slice."

Even though I was full, my mouth watered as my

gaze scanned the wide variety of baked goods. When I spotted a plate piled high with double chocolate chip cookies, I groaned, "Please tell me those don't taste as good as they look."

Kian shook his head. "Sorry, no can do. Lucy makes some of the best cookies I've ever had."

"I think you meant to say *the* best," Dom growled, leaning between us to grab one of the cookies. Popping it into his mouth, he strolled away to return to his wife's side. Lucy rolled her eyes with a smile.

Laughing softly, I picked up a cookie. "With an endorsement like that, I guess I can make room for just one."

"I think we can do better than that." He took two more from the plate and wrapped them in a napkin before shoving them into a pocket on the inside of his leather vest, sending a shiver down my spine when his fingers brushed against the underside of my breast. "There, you can eat these whenever you're hungry later."

"Did I just see you put cookies in your concealed carry pocket?" Mac grumbled.

"Yup." Kian flashed him an unrepentant grin and shrugged. "I didn't want Tessa to miss out, so I snagged a couple of extras for her."

"Good call."

I would've been shocked by the Silver Saints president's easy acceptance of Kian's explanation, except I'd seen how he was with his wife and kids. He was a big, tough guy on the outside, but he was a giant softie when it came to his family.

"Sorry, but I need to drag you away from Tessa."

Kian started to shake his head, but I waved them away. "Go ahead. I'm more than fine. I'll go compliment Lucy on her cookies while you're busy."

"I won't be too long," Kian promised.

"Sorry, Tessa."

It turned out that the apologetic smile Mac aimed at me was about more than just pulling Kian away for a quick conversation during the barbecue, which I found out a few hours later when I followed him up to his room. The large space was surprisingly clean but sparsely furnished with just a king-sized bed, dresser, recliner, and bedside table. And a giant flat-screen television—exactly what one would expect in a bachelor pad.

"We're...um...staying here?"

"It isn't much, but it's what I've been calling home since I joined the Silver Saints. Which turned out to be a good call because you can pick out the new place and it's a buyer's market right now. Great timing." While I was wrapping my head around him trusting me to choose his next home, he strode to the closet and grabbed a pair of sweatpants and a T-shirt. "Go ahead and get ready for bed. I need to do a couple of things first."

Feeling nervous about sharing a bed with a man for the first time, I took longer in the bathroom than I normally would have. When I finally came out, I spotted a duffel bag near the door, and surprise replaced my worry. "Are we going somewhere else?"

"Not we. You're gonna stay here while I take care of something for Mac."

My shoulders slumped, and I ducked my head while I thought about how to respond to this news. I was so disappointed that Kian was leaving, but I had no right to ask him not to go. Although he'd brought me here, he didn't owe me anything.

"Hey now, sweet girl." He pressed a finger against my chin to tilt my head back until I stared into his blue eyes. "I'm as disappointed as you are. You have no idea how much I wanted to tell my prez that he had to find someone else to handle this particular club business, but there isn't anyone else as equipped to handle it as me. I hope you understand that I can't let them down."

Somehow, Kian had become my safe place in

such a short amount of time. Knowing he was willing to honor his commitment to the Silver Saints, even when it meant sacrificing what he wanted, only reinforced he was the kind of man I could trust.

And although I didn't want to be separated from him so soon, the last thing I wanted was to distract him while he was doing something potentially dangerous. So I put on a brave face and murmured, "I'm not going to lie and say the timing doesn't suck, but it'll be okay. Everyone has been so nice to me. I'm sure I'll be fine staying here without you."

"You'll be more than fine, Tessa. Nobody gets into the compound without our say-so, and Mac will stick close and keep an eye out for me." He cupped my face, his thumb stroking my cheek. "Which means Bridget will be here too, so you'll have someone to hang out with. Some of the other guys and their old ladies, too."

"Then it sounds like I'll have plenty of distractions until you return." My nose wrinkled. "But when do you need to leave? Right now?"

He shook his head. "Not until early morning."

"Oh, good." My relief over having a little more time with him dispelled my nervousness over spending the night in bed together. "You should try to get some rest then."

"I could say the same. It's been a long couple of days for you." He tugged me over to the bed and helped me settle on my good side. Then he gently wrapped his arms around me, being careful not to put any pressure on my ribs.

Being cradled in his embrace was even better than I imagined. "This is nice."

"Fucking perfect," he rasped, his breath hot against my neck. "Hate to ruin the moment, but I need to update you on your college fund before I leave."

Twisting my neck to look at him, I laughed softly. "It hasn't even been a full day yet, and the bank is closed, but you already have an update?"

"When you have someone like Grey on your side, you don't have to worry about business hours. He put his hacking skills to good use and set up an untraceable bank account for you. Then he transferred every last penny from your college savings into it, so nobody can touch the money except for you," he explained. "So now you have time to figure out what you want to do without anyone pressuring you into making a decision you might regret later."

"I really appreciate him taking a risk like that for me. Thank you."

Knowing that I had options was a relief, but I

couldn't help but wonder how bad things would get for my dad if I didn't give him the money.

"Anything for you." Pulling me closer, he brushed his lips against mine in the briefest of kisses.

Before he could pull away, I cupped the back of his head and whispered, "More. I want my first real kiss to be a good one."

"Fuck," he groaned, his mouth crashing against mine as he proceeded to blow my mind by exceeding my wildest imagination of what a kiss could be. Our tongues tangled together while he cradled me gently against his chest, his palm stroking my side before his fingers dug into my hip.

When he finally lifted his head, I was in a dazed fog. "Wow."

"Rest easy, sweet girl. I've got your back."

While that was both literally and figuratively true since he was spooning me, I drifted off to sleep faster than I had in months.

8

PHANTOM

I stared at my reflection in the mirror, inspecting the growth on the lower half of my face. Inside the medicine cabinet was a razor and shaving cream, and I debated whether to use it.

The night I had to leave, Tessa had looked hot as fuck in one of my T-shirts, and it had taken every ounce of my control to simply hold her while she slept and not take it any farther. But I wasn't going to rush through our first time together. When I left at four o'clock the next morning, I kissed her forehead and whispered that I loved her and to be safe.

The only reason I felt comfortable leaving her at all was because we kept the compound locked down tight. And Mac had promised to stay at the clubhouse, along with a couple of other brothers who knew multiple ways to kill a person, until I returned. He'd also agreed to one more favor—I asked him to have Tessa's property patch and vest ready when I got home.

I'd just returned after being gone for four days and headed straight to my bathroom to take a shower. It was only around midnight, but Tessa was fast asleep in my bed. All I wanted to do was crawl in there with her, but I wouldn't do that without washing away the filth from the past four days. Literally and figuratively.

After a frigid shower, I had planned to shave, but something stopped me. After a few minutes, I admitted the truth to myself. I wouldn't be able to hold back from Tessa for much longer. When I finally took her cherry, I wanted to see my whisker burn all over her silky skin, branding her on the outside the same way I intended to on the inside.

Quietly, I opened the bathroom door, quickly shutting off the light so it wouldn't wake her, then I padded naked over to the bed and slipped under the covers. Tessa immediately rolled toward me, plastering herself against my side with a soft sigh.

I was pleased when I didn't see her wince at the movement because I'd been worried about her pain. Patch had kept me informed, but I would always want to see to her care myself, so it bugged the fuck out of me that I wasn't there.

Tessa snuggled even closer, throwing a leg across mine and an arm over my chest. Her knee bumped my groin, and I groaned at the sharp pain that shot through my hard, swollen cock.

The sound must have woken her because she froze, then slowly raised her head and blinked sleepily. "Kian?" she whispered.

"Hey, sweet girl," I murmured, bending my head down to brush my lips over hers.

When I retreated, she had a dreamy smile on her gorgeous face. "Welcome home." Then her cheeks heated as her gaze dropped to my chest. "I missed you."

I wrapped a hand around her thigh and held her leg around me as I rolled us so she was on her back, and I hovered above her. "Missed you, too, baby."

She gasped when I dropped down on top of her, pressing our bodies together and nestling my hard-on in the apex of her thighs. "Barely thought about anything besides getting back to you," I growled. "Dying to feel your skin against mine, to be inside you, to hear you scream my name. Can't fucking wait to get inside your tight virgin pussy and take your cherry. Gonna make you mine."

Tessa's face was flushed, and her eyes were filled with desire, but she still looked adorably shy. "I... um...I want that, too."

I stared into her jade pools, making sure she didn't miss the intensity of my next words. "Once I get inside you, there's no going back, sweet girl. You'll be mine. Only mine. Understand?"

She nodded, but that wasn't enough for me. "I want to hear you say it, Tessa."

"I'm yours," she breathed, tightening the leg curled around my waist.

"All fucking mine," I grunted before I slammed my mouth down onto hers.

The moment our lips touched, need raced through me like a forest fire. I had to get her naked. *Now*.

Without losing our connection, I lifted my hips, reached between us, and grasped her panties, tearing them away. Then I slipped my hands under my shirt that she'd worn and gently glided them up her torso, pushing the hem up over her tits. Ripping my mouth from hers, I smirked at her whimper of protest, which turned into a yelp when I wrapped my lips around one of her pink nipples.

I suckled the bud while I shoved the shirt the rest of the way up and pulled it off, tossing it over the side of the bed. When I lowered my body, my skin sizzled anywhere we touched, and I groaned in bliss. My fingers twisted and plucked her other stiff peak, and I rocked my big cock against her pussy.

"Kian!" she gasped, and her other leg curled around my waist.

I switched sides as I continued to rock against her until I felt my dick sliding easily through her soaked pussy lips.

"So fucking wet," I rasped when I released her nipple with a pop. I returned to her mouth, pushing my tongue inside and exploring her decadent taste.

She'd become so slick that my long, fat cock parted her folds and rubbed her clit, making her clench her legs and moan. When the tip bumped against her entrance, I knew I needed to stop. She wasn't ready for my invasion yet.

I pulled away, and she chased my lips with a frustrated grunt, then glared at me while I took her legs from around me and spread them as wide as they would comfortably go. Smirking, I winked and slowly moved down her body, kissing each nipple before licking a ring around her belly button, then settled my shoulders between her thighs.

"Fuck, you're gorgeous," I rasped as my eyes feasted on the sight of her drenched and swollen pink pussy. Licking my lips in anticipation, I glanced up when she tensed.

"Relax, baby," I crooned. "Do you trust me?"

Her immediate nod caused warmth to spread through my chest, and I kissed each of her thighs to let her know her response pleased me. Then I parted her southern lips and licked her from bottom to top, though I carefully avoided her little bundle of nerves.

"Kian!" she gasped as her hands tunneled through my hair. Her hands clutched my head as if to keep me from pulling away. Yeah, that was not fucking happening. Her pussy was the sweetest thing I'd ever tasted, and I was officially addicted.

I lapped at her center over and over, coming close to but never touching her clit. When she was strung tighter than a drum and begging for more, I sucked the hard little nub into my mouth just as I plunged a finger into her channel. It was a tight fit, and I worried she might not stretch enough to take my whole length and girth. But she was fucking made for me, so I tossed the worry away and focused on priming her for my invasion.

My cheeks hollowed out as I sucked and curled my finger up to graze her most sensitive inner spot. Tessa screamed and splintered apart. Her muscles clamped around my digit, and her pussy flooded my mouth with her sweet nectar. I didn't wait for her to come down from her climax before I started working her toward another and managed to get a second finger inside her. When she came again, I slipped in a third.

"Fuck," I grunted. "Gonna squeeze the fuck outta my dick, sweet girl. Can't wait to fuck you deep and feel you come around me. Gonna fill this virgin pussy with so much come you'll be dripping for days."

"Kian," she moaned. "It's too much. I can't take any more."

"You will," I commanded.

I removed my fingers from her sex and crawled back up her body, wrapping her legs around me again and positioning my tip at her entrance. My mouth captured hers in a deep kiss as I slowly pushed inside her, stopping frequently to let her stretch to accommodate my size. Her inner muscles clenched, and pleasure streaked from my dick to my balls, making them tingle. I wasn't going to last long.

Steeling up my control, I worked in another inch as I kissed my way from her mouth and down her neck to her tits. Tessa arched her back and tightened her legs, making me groan in ecstasy. Suddenly, I felt resistance and stopped, releasing her nipple and concentrating hard on staying still so I didn't rip her to shreds by shoving my dick balls deep in one explosive thrust.

"Relax, baby," I told her softly. I fucking hated that I had to hurt her, but nothing would stop me from making her mine.

I slipped a hand between us and manipulated her clit until she undulated against me, crying out in need. Finally, I dove in, breaking through her barrier and burying myself from root to tip, then used every bit of my energy to stop. It was the hardest fucking thing I'd ever done.

But the tears on her cheeks when I looked at her tugged at my heart, and I forgot about everything except her pain. I wiped them away with my thumbs before cradling her beautiful face between my palms and kissing her tenderly. "I'm sorry, sweet girl."

Tessa took a deep breath and gave me a watery smile. "It's feeling better now. I feel…um, stretched and, um, really full."

I clenched my jaw, barely restraining myself while I waited for her to give me the green light. "You're killing me, Tessa," I gritted out.

"I think…would…would you move?"

"Fuck, yes," I growled before withdrawing a couple of inches and sliding back in.

"Yessss," she moaned, pressing her head back into the pillow. "More."

This time, I pulled out to the tip, then slammed back in, shouting at the bliss that filled me when her pussy throbbed around my cock.

She gasped, and my eyes shot to her face, seeing her slight wince.

"Fuck!" I growled. "Did I hurt you?"

Tessa looked as if she might lie, but when she saw the dark expression on my face, she muttered, "Just a little. My ribs are still a tiny bit sore."

"Shit." I had to stop, but I didn't know how the fuck I was going to find the strength.

"Please, Kian," she begged, gliding her hands down my back to grip my ass. "Don't stop. It feels better than it hurts. Please. I need you."

Hearing her beg for my dick and the breathy way she said my name scattered my thoughts.

"Tell me if it becomes too much," I grunted. When she nodded, I moved again, slowly dragging my cock out and then gently gliding back in. My jaw was clenched so tight from holding back that I wouldn't have been surprised if I cracked a tooth.

"I won't break, Kian," she whispered in my ear. "Fuck me."

Her words sent all the blood left in my body drained to my cock. Just enough sanity remained so that I was aware of her ribs, but my primal instincts took over.

"So fucking sexy when you beg, sweet girl. You want my cock fucking this tight pussy until you can't walk without feeling me inside you?"

"Yesss," she hissed, squeezing her channel and milking my dick, bringing me closer to orgasm.

"That's it, baby. Take me all the way. Wanna hear you screaming my name. Fuck! Yes, Tessa! Fuck!"

"Yes, yes! Oh, Kian!" Tessa cried out, her nails digging into my ass cheeks as her hips bucked up to meet each thrust.

It suddenly hit me that I was bare inside her, but before I could even consider pulling out, the Neanderthal inside me roared at the idea of breeding my woman. I wanted Tessa tied to me in every way, and the image of my woman sporting a swollen belly had come spurting from my cock.

"Are you on birth control?" I growled as I continued to pound her pussy, driving her higher.

"What...? Oh, gosh. Oh, yes!"

She blinked a few times, trying to clear away the fog, but I wouldn't let up my pace, making sure she wasn't thinking clearly. It was an asshole move, but I wouldn't let her stop me from getting what I wanted.

"Birth control," I grunted again.

"Um...no...I—oh, oh...Kian! Yes! Yes!"

Knowing her womb was unprotected filled me with satisfaction, and I knew I wouldn't last any longer.

Tessa writhed with passion, close to peaking, so I sucked on one of her nipples as I reached between us and pinched her clit. She threw her head back and screamed my name, sending me over the edge with her.

I shouted in ecstasy and exploded inside her, shooting jet after jet of hot come into her ripe body. It seemed impossible that I could have so much seed, filling her until it leaked and dripped down her thighs. But it just kept coming until I finally collapsed on top of her, empty and utterly spent.

Mindful of my weight and her ribs, I held her close as I rolled to my back, keeping her on top of me and my still hard cock buried inside her.

"Mine," I grunted as I held her close, her body fitting perfectly into mine. "You're mine."

"Yours," she agreed softly, filling me with that warmth again.

We stayed like that for a while, but I knew she'd be even more sore if I didn't take care of her. So I eventually pulled out and padded over to the bathroom, cleaning myself before taking a warm, wet cloth out and tenderly caring for her. When I spotted the whisker burns on her thighs, around her tits, and several other spots, I almost said fuck it and took her again. However, I didn't want to cause her more pain, and I doubted her ribs could take another round any more than her pussy.

So I climbed into bed and pulled her into my arms, holding her close as we fell asleep.

9

TESSA

I'd grown comfortable in the Silver Saints clubhouse over the past four days without Kian, but waking up wrapped in his arms made his room my favorite place ever. Especially after the orgasms he'd given me last night.

Kian had definitely left his mark on my body. In more ways than one.

My rib pain was basically almost gone, but I felt twinges in other places this morning. A small sound escaped my lips as I rolled over, and Kian's eyes popped open. "You okay, baby?"

"Yeah," I sighed, burying my face against his broad chest as I was overcome with shyness. I'd been entirely on board with giving him my virginity last night, but I felt a little awkward and unsure how to act in the cold light of day.

Luckily for me, Kian didn't seem to have the same problem. Kissing my temple, he murmured, "Never been happier to be back home after taking care of club business. Coming back to you in my bed in nothing but my shirt is something I could get used to."

"Keep waking me up that way, and I'll wear whatever you want to bed," I mumbled.

With my lips pressed against his skin, and my voice pitched low, my words were barely audible, but he proved to have excellent hearing since he chuckled and replied, "Then we're both gonna be happy as fuck because I fully plan to make it a habit."

"I guess we have a plan." My stomach let out a rumble, and my cheeks heated even more.

"Sounds like I better feed you." He gave me a quick kiss. "You're gonna need energy for later."

I peeked up at him, liking the sound of that. "I am, huh?"

"Definitely."

He kissed me again before sliding off the mattress and tugging me with him. Since I hadn't bothered to put his shirt back on after we had sex, I was completely naked. Something Kian took full advantage of before I could cover up.

Palming the underside of my breast, he brushed his thumb over my pebbled nipple while his other hand drifted to my butt. "Then again, coming home to you without a stitch on might be even better, sweet girl."

"Um…I'm not sure I'm ready for that." Or that I ever would be while staying here. "It would be just my luck that there would be a fire or something, and I'd have to run past all your club brothers without any clothes on."

"Fuck, good point." He lightly swatted my butt. "Nobody gets to see you like this but me."

Butterflies swirled in my belly at his possessive tone. "You won't get any argument from me."

"Because you're mine."

"Yours," I confirmed, enjoying hearing him say it now as much as I had when he was taking my virginity.

"Which means I get to take care of you." He winked at me, and I giggled. "So breakfast first, devouring your pussy later."

I fanned my face with my hand. "Like I said before, I'm not going to argue with that plan."

We got dressed—Cat had brought about a dozen

shopping bags to the clubhouse when she found out I had only brought a few things with me—and headed down to the kitchen. For the past four mornings, it had been packed with club members, their wives, and their children. But today, we only found Mac, Bridget, and their son Dane sitting at the table.

"Good morning, you two," Bridget chirped, her lips curving into a big grin. "Now I get why everyone else headed home right after breakfast—Phantom is back."

Kian nodded. "Got in late last night."

"And thank fuck for that." Mac got up and slapped him on the back. "Hated to send you out just when you found your girl. Know it sucks that we got to know her before you really got the chance, but I gotta say—you chose well."

"You really did," Bridget agreed with a soft smile. "Tessa fit right in with all of us like she's been here forever, but it was clear that she missed you."

Kian tugged me against his side and brushed a kiss against the top of my head. "Not as much as I missed her."

"How about I make you guys a batch of French toast as a thank you for the time you sacrificed on behalf of the club?" Bridget offered.

Kian patted his six-pack abs. "If you want to

make them, I'll be happy to eat them. But you don't owe me anything for doing my part."

"And that right there is part of why Tessa is a lucky girl for finding you." Bridget rolled her eyes at Mac's growl, going up on her toes to kiss him on the cheek before she started cracking eggs into a bowl and whisking them with milk, vanilla, and cinnamon.

"Can I have some too, Mom?" Dane asked.

"How in the world are you hungry again?" Bridget shook her head as she pulled out a loaf of bread. "You just had breakfast half an hour ago."

Her son shrugged. "What can I say? I'm a growing boy."

"Damn straight you are, my little man," Mac agreed.

Dane puffed his little chest out. "I'm gonna be as big as you someday, and then when I'm old enough, I'm gonna be prez just like you too."

Kian squeezed the boy's shoulder. "If you work hard enough, I can see you following in your dad's footsteps."

Dane crossed his thin arms over his chest, mimicking Mac's stance. "Good, because I'm gonna."

"Keep that confidence. You're gonna need it." Kian chuckled and shook his head. "Where are the girls?"

"Molly went over to Silver Ink to show Uncle Nova something she drew." Dane rolled his eyes. "Dahlia and Callie trailed her."

Kian ruffled the boy's hair. "You didn't want to go with them?"

"Nah, I wanted to hang with Dad instead."

Mac smiled down at him. "That's my boy."

Watching how the eleven-year-old tried to emulate his father and Kian made me smile. As much as I enjoyed seeing Kian with Cat's daughter Opal on my first day here, seeing him interact with Dane now hit me a little harder—but in the best way possible.

My reaction was probably because there hadn't been anything between us when we had sex, which meant that I could already be pregnant. Especially with how much come he'd stuffed me with. It had been dripping down my thighs before he'd washed me with a warm, damp cloth. Since we hadn't known each other long—and had spent most of that time texting each other while he was gone—I most likely should've been appalled by the risk I'd taken. Instead, I found myself too easily picturing Kian as the father of my children.

"You doing okay, sweet girl?" Kian asked.

I nodded. "Uh-huh."

Bridget sent me a knowing look, and I remembered the meet-cute story she'd shared with me. And how little time passed between when Mac kidnapped her and when she got pregnant with Molly.

Her life turned out amazing, so if Kian had already knocked me up, I hoped mine would too. With all the wild things that happened when so many of the other Silver Saints couples met, my story seemed mild in comparison. The only thing that really stood in our way now was my dad's situation with his bookie and the fact that I was supposed to be headed back to college soon.

But now that I found Kian and had fallen for him, I was pretty sure that I had decided what to do about school. Although education was important to my mom, all she ever wanted was for me to be happy. And being with Kian gave me more joy than I'd felt in a long time. The possibility of spending the rest of my life with him—and raising a family—filled me with excitement while the thought of returning to school only left me feeling anxious. Especially since it meant being away from Kian.

10

PHANTOM

"Fuck, yes, sweet girl. Ride me, take me deep. Fuck!"

"Oh, Kian! Yes!"

Tessa's head dropped back, and her long auburn hair tickled my thighs as she bounced on my dick. I cupped her big tits, filling my hands and massaging them while I bucked my hips to meet her every time she dropped.

Her pace increased, and I pinched her nipples, making her cry out as her movements became wild and frantic. She looked like a goddess above me, and if I hadn't been so consumed with passion, I might have taken a second to revel in awe that she belonged to me.

But at that moment, I couldn't focus on anything

except her pussy clutching my dick like it never wanted to let go...and my determination to knock her up. I grasped her hips and slammed her down onto my cock a few more times before she exploded with a scream that rang off the walls.

I roared her name as I followed her over the edge, and my body convulsed with the strength of my climax.

"You are so fucking sexy, baby," I breathed as I stared at her gorgeous, naked body sitting astride mine.

She fell onto my chest as if she had no energy to hold herself up. I knew exactly how she felt. But even if I'd been able to move, I didn't want to. I held her close, my dick still sheathed in her channel, keeping as much of my come as possible from leaking out.

I could feel her heartbeat against my chest, and it began to slow, becoming in sync with mine.

"I could say the same about you," she panted.

A smile stretched across my face, and I hugged her before rolling us over so she was on her back. "Tell me you're mine, sweet girl."

Tessa giggled, probably because it was a frequent demand of mine. "I'm yours, Kian."

"Fucking right," I agreed. "And I want every motherfucker who looks at you to know it."

She laughed and hugged me tightly. "I'm not getting your name tattooed on my forehead, Kian," she muttered teasingly. I'd joked about it a few times, although I did love the idea of my name inked on her silky skin somewhere on her body.

However, that wasn't a big enough statement to warn away other men.

Forcing myself to leave her perfect warmth, I withdrew—smirking when she whimpered in protest—and climbed off the bed. I padded over to the closet where someone had hung my present for Tessa. First, I reached up to the top shelf and retrieved the surprise I'd brought back a couple of days ago. I put it in the vest pocket before removing it from the hanger. Then I shut the door and made my way back to the bed, holding the cut at my side. Once I was standing next to it, I crooked my finger at my woman. "C'mere, sweet girl."

She hadn't quite gotten over her shyness in the bedroom—despite her uninhibited behavior once she lost herself to our passion—so she wrapped the sheet around her before scooting to the edge of the bed.

I held out my hand, and she took it, letting me help her to her feet. Then I grabbed the sheet and yanked, ripping it away from her. She gasped and moved to cover herself, but I glared at her until she dropped her hands to her sides. "Don't hide your body from me, Tessa," I growled. "You're mine, and when I want to see your sexy body, you will show it to me. *Mine*."

Her cheeks bloomed with pink, but the corners of her mouth lifted, and she nodded.

"I want you to wear this, sweet girl." I held up the leather vest, first showing her the back, which was taken up by the Silver Saints patch, along with the words, "Property of Phantom."

Tessa's mouth opened into a surprised little O, and she looked from it to me, her eyes wide and questioning. "You want me to be your old lady?"

I rolled my eyes and turned the cut around to show her that her name was stitched on the front. "Did you really think I wouldn't ask the woman I love to be my old lady? I've claimed you, and I'm doing my best to knock you the fuck up. Of course I want you to wear my property patch."

Holding up the vest, I gestured for her to turn around so I could slip it up her arms and settle it on her shoulders. When I turned her back around, I smiled with satisfaction. Then I quirked an eyebrow when I saw her glazed eyes and the stunned look on her face.

"You love me?" she whispered, her mouth spreading into a beautiful smile.

Hadn't I told her that...? *Well, shit.* I'd only said it to her when she was asleep. Settling my hands on her hips, I pulled her close until her front was plastered to mine. "I love you more than anything in this world, Tessa."

Her jade-green orbs suddenly swam in tears, and I panicked until she beamed at me. "I love you, too!"

"Fucking, right," I agreed before dropping my head and giving her a searing kiss that made her toes curl. When I released her lips, I growled, "Need you. Gonna fuck you while you're wearing my brand."

I picked her up and tossed her onto the bed but stopped when she yelped and sat up. She frowned down at her vest, and that was when I remembered what I'd put in the pocket. She must have landed on the hard little box.

After checking one side, she looked at the other and spotted the bulge, then took out the contents. Her brow rose as she stared at the velvet box, then her jaw dropped, and her head whipped up, her eyes meeting mine.

I grinned and sat on the bed, taking the box and flipping up the lid to reveal a sparkling diamond ring. "Told you I want everyone who sees you to know you're taken. And I want you bound to me in every way."

"Are you asking me to marry you?"

I frowned and took the ring from the box, then grabbed her hand and slipped it on her finger. "Fuck no. I'm telling you. We are getting married."

"Is that so?" she asked sassily.

I grinned and threw the box over my shoulder before shoving her back against the mattress and coming down over her. "Say yes, sweet girl. Or I'm gonna make you scream it until you pass out from orgasms."

Tessa smirked before miming zipping her lips and throwing away the key.

"Orgasms it is."

I slid down her body until my mouth was level with her glistening pussy, and I stared up at her with a wicked smile. "I'll tell you what. If I can make you scream yes...let's say... a dozen times in the next hour, I get to pick how many kids we have."

Tessa giggled until she realized I wasn't laughing. Then she narrowed her eyes and a determined gleam entered them. "Fine. But if I win, I get a year to plan our wedding."

Fuck that. No way in hell would I wait a year to marry her.

"So I've been thinking..." Tessa mused, tapping her fingers on my chest.

"About the wedding you have to plan in four weeks?" I asked smugly.

Tessa huffed, shimmying her body and making my dick twitch inside her. She quickly rolled off me, causing me to scowl at the loss of her warmth and snug pussy.

She sat up and pulled the sheet over her tits, then rolled her eyes when I raised an eyebrow and let it fall back to her waist.

"I want to give the money to my dad."

"What the fuck?" I jackknifed up and stared at her like she'd lost her mind because, clearly, she had.

"Hear me out." I opened my mouth to argue, but her lips formed an adorable little pout, and she pleaded, "Please?"

Pussy whipped. Like so many of my brothers. "I'm listening."

"My education was really important to my mom, and if she were here, I'd probably finish school just to make her happy. But the truth is, I don't want to go back. That isn't what will make me happy."

I sighed and grabbed her hips, hauling her onto my lap so she straddled my legs. "What will make you happy, sweet girl?"

"You. Being your old lady, your wife, and the mother of our…"

To my utter shock, my words got stuck in my throat, and I felt a little choked up. I swallowed hard and rasped, "Six, maybe eight…depending on how sexy you are when you're pregnant."

"Mother of our *four* kids."

I narrowed my eyes, and she giggled. "We'll discuss that later. Go on about the money."

"Despite what my dad has become, I don't want to see him come to any harm. I'll hold on to my childhood memories and hope the money gives him a fresh start."

"You are too fucking good for that asshole," I growled. Then I gave her a quick, hard kiss, and sighed. "Too fucking good for me, too, but I'm never letting you go."

"I can call him—"

"I will agree to this on one condition," I interrupted her, knowing she was about to offer to contact her dad…and probably go see the bookie for herself.

That thought made me shudder. "I'll handle getting the money to the people he owes."

"Okay," she whispered with a sweet smile. "Thank you."

"No need to thank me, sweet girl. I've got your back. Always."

11

TESSA

"I know you do, which is why I feel good about this decision." I brushed my lips against his. "Because I know I don't need the money as a backup plan when I have you."

He captured my mouth in a deep kiss that left me panting. "You're so damn sweet. Is it any wonder I fell in love with you?"

Butterflies swirled in my belly. "You make it easy."

"I need a taste of the sweetest part of you." He bucked his hips up, his hard length pressing against my core. "Speak now or forever hold your peace."

I shook my head with a giggle. "I think that line is for the wedding."

"Sorry, but that's the only time you'll hear it."

Flipping me onto my back, he levered himself over my body. "No way in hell am I going to give anyone the chance to put a stop to our wedding. We're going to skip that part on our big day."

"Well, you definitely don't need to worry that I'm going to say I don't want your mouth on me." I pressed my inner thighs together. "Even after you've made me scream your name so many times, I still want you. I swear, you've turned me into some kind of sex fiend. I always want you."

"We can be sex fiends together, then," he rasped, his hand moving between us to stroke his dick. "All I have to do is think about you, and I'm hard as a fucking rock. My cock just won't go down when I'm near you."

Feeling bold now that I knew he loved me, I wrapped my hand around his and squeezed. "Then we should put it to good use. Again."

"Whatever you want, sweet girl." He nipped at my neck and added, "Especially if it's my dick."

I was having fun with all of the sexual innuendo, but I lost my train of thought when he sucked one of my puckered nipples into his mouth. Teasing quickly turned to passion, and I thrust my fingers into his hair to tug his head closer.

When he let the pebbled peak pop out of his mouth, I mewled in protest. "Please don't stop."

"Don't worry, sweet girl. I'm gonna keep going until you've screamed my name another dozen times," he reassured me, a sexy smirk curving his lips. "Seems like the perfect way to celebrate the fact that we're getting married in a month."

I pressed my lips together to stop myself from confessing that I would've happily faked each one of those orgasms if it meant I got to marry him sooner rather than later. But it sure as heck had been fun letting him convince me. Just like our engagement celebration would be.

He shifted his attention to the other side, and I squirmed beneath him, beyond turned on. Licking and sucking my breasts, he rocked his hard length against my core.

"I'm already so close, Kian. Please," I panted.

"Love how sensitive your tits are." He cupped the rounded globes and pressed them together, running his tongue through the valley between them. "Can't fucking wait to see if I can make you come just by playing with them when you're pregnant."

I loved how easily he talked about our future together—from our wedding to babies and everything in between. "With all the unprotected sex we've been having, you probably won't need to wait too long."

"Fuck, I hope you're right." His intense blue eyes burned with desire, his love shining brightly from them as well.

"Even if I'm not, we'll have all the fun practicing until it happens."

"Damn straight." He circled my nipple with his tongue before kissing his way down my stomach. "Starting now."

He grabbed my ankles and spread my legs as wide as they would go before pressing them back slightly. The position left me wide open to his gaze, but my shyness had apparently been overcome by him confessing his love for me because I didn't try to cover myself.

"That's my sweet girl," he murmured approvingly. "Show me that pretty pussy that's mine and only mine."

"You saying 'mine' in that deep voice of yours is one of the biggest turn-ons ever. It turns me on so much," I confessed.

He flashed me a cocky grin. "That's a lucky thing since you're gonna hear it for the rest of your life."

Any response I might have given was drowned out by my moan when he spread my pussy lips and licked up the center. Then he wrapped my hands around my ankles so I'd hold myself open for him, and my pleasure ratcheted up another notch.

Lowering his mouth over my swollen mound again, he buried his face in my pussy and devoured me until I screamed his name until my throat was hoarse. This release was the most powerful I'd experienced, leaving me feeling like I was melting into the mattress.

"Holy heck, I don't know if I can take any more."

"I know you can, sweet girl." He lined up his dick with my drenched pussy. "Right?"

"Uh-huh." I cradled his hips between my thighs, my heels digging into his butt as I urged him closer. The groan that rumbled up his chest when he began to slide inside my snug channel just about triggered another orgasm all by itself—that was how sexy he sounded.

I loved knowing that I had the power to bring this powerful man to the brink of his control. That I could push him over the edge. Being the woman he loved. The one he was going to spend the rest of his life with.

"I was wrong. I need you again. Please, Kian."

He inched his hips forward until the tip of his dick was notched inside my entrance. "Thank fuck, baby, because I need to feel your perfect pussy wrapped around my cock almost more than I need to breathe right now."

Twining my arms around his neck, I whispered, "Then take me."

"Always," he rasped, driving his hips forward in one powerful thrust until he was fully lodged inside me.

It didn't matter that we'd done this at least a dozen times since that first night. Each time he sank into my tight heat, it took me a moment to adjust to his invasion. He was just so thick and long.

"Damn, you're almost as tight as the night I popped your cherry, sweet girl," he grunted.

"Kian," I moaned, my head thrashing from side to side as my inner walls clenched around his hard length.

He gave me a moment for the stretching sensation to pass before he circled his hips. "You ready for more now?"

"Yesss," I hissed.

"Thank fuck." He retreated a few inches and bucked his hips hard, thrusting right back in. "Gonna take you fast and hard."

"Please." Knowing what I was in for, I gripped his shoulders and held on tight for the ride. He quickly picked up the pace until he did exactly as promised, pounding me into the mattress harder than ever.

Now that my ribs weren't sore anymore, he didn't have to hold back, and I finally got to feel the full power of his muscular body as he hammered in and out of me.

"So fucking perfect." His gaze was locked between our bodies as he watched his dick sink inside me.

The stark sensuality in his masculine face and the burning need in his blue orbs just about put me over the edge again. "So close."

"That's it, sweet girl." He wedged his arm between our bodies and started to circle my clit with his thumb. "Come for me."

All it took was another couple of thrusts of his hips, and then I was screaming his name even louder than before. "Yes! Kian! Oh, yes!"

"Tessa! Fuck, baby! Your pussy milks my cock so fucking good," he growled, his hips continuing to pump even as his dick twitched inside me and hot spurts of come splashed against my inner walls. His release triggered an aftershock for me, and I trembled in his arms until he finally stopped moving and collapsed against me with a groan. "Holy fuck, baby.

If that's what engagement sex is like, I can't fucking wait to see how incredible married sex is gonna be."

"Then I guess it's a good thing you talked me into a short engagement," I teased, cuddling against his chest after he rolled onto his back.

"Talked you into it?" he echoed with a chuckle. "Is that what I did?"

"That's the story I'm going to tell our children when they're older, so yeah." I gestured at our naked bodies. "I wouldn't want to scar them for life with what really happened."

"That's probably a good call." His palm glided down my spine. "But they're going to be so used to seeing their parents kiss that they won't be the least bit surprised that I couldn't keep my hands off you."

I loved the sound of that. "Something to look forward to."

12

PHANTOM

"Breaker," I greeted our Sergeant at Arms when he walked into Mac's office a couple of days after I returned.

"Hey," he replied with a nod before taking a seat on one of the couches in the corner of the office.

Mac nodded at me, giving me permission to lead the meeting now that all of our enforcers were present.

I looked at Grey and sighed. "Tessa wants to give the money to her dad."

His brows shot up, but he didn't comment.

I rolled my eyes to the ceiling with my jaw clenched and gritted out, "She wants to clear his debt so he doesn't end up hurt or worse."

"Gonna do it?" Nova asked.

"Why not just mail the check to the jackass?" suggested Dom.

"You think he'd actually give it up or try to run away with it, which would get his ass six feet under?" I asked dryly.

He grunted in agreement.

"Gonna take the money straight to the bookie. And make sure he spreads the word that no one is to lend to him from now on. Tessa's dad wants to get in trouble again, it won't be here, where it could get back to my woman."

"The shit we do for our women," Patch groaned.

"Nova, Dom, Breaker, Grey, go with him," Mac ordered. "Hack, I want you in contact with Grey. They balk at our show of force, Grey can threaten shit, and you can show 'em we mean business."

There was a chorus of agreements, then we all arranged to meet at the garage in thirty.

"Scout, Knight, and I will cover you from a distance, especially while you have the cash."

I nodded my thanks, then ran upstairs to talk to Tessa.

She was just stepping out of the shower, and I had to force myself to remember that my brothers were waiting, and I didn't have time to fuck my woman right now.

"Got club business, sweet girl. I'll be back in a few hours."

"Okay," she replied with a pretty smile.

She didn't ask where I was going or what I was doing, knowing I couldn't answer. Her easy acceptance of my life just made me love her even more.

I strode over and gave her a panty-melting kiss, then growled, "I want you naked and waiting for me in bed when I get back."

Tessa shivered, but her expression was sassy when she answered, "I might have stuff to do, Kian."

"I'll text you when I'm headed home." I curled my fingers into the wet hair on the back of her head and yanked it back. "Naked. Bed."

"And if I'm not?"

"Your ass will be so red you won't be able to sit tomorrow."

Tessa swallowed hard, and I almost grinned at the indecision in her eyes.

"Gotta go." I gave her another quick kiss, then turned to leave but stopped when she grabbed my cut.

"Be safe and come home to me," she said when I looked back at her.

"Nothing will stop me from coming home to you, sweet girl."

By the time I got down to the garage, I was in a shit mood. The last thing I wanted to be doing was leaving my wet, naked old lady in our bed without me.

"Need to get this the fuck over with," I grumbled. "Let's ride."

Hack had located the address for the club where Don Falco kept shop. It was a dirty strip joint on the outskirts of town. Just parking my bike in front of it made me feel slimy.

I waited for my brothers to dismount, then led the way to the door, passing by the line of scantily dressed women and greasy men. The bouncer was a football has-been who'd come by his muscles artificially. When he spotted us, he straightened to his full height—which was several inches shorter than most of us—and tried to look intimidating.

"There's a line, assholes," he grunted.

"Get the fuck outta the way," I ordered in a menacing tone.

The bouncer swallowed, then glanced at our audience and tried again. "Get to the back of the line or leave."

I closed the distance between us and looked down at him. "You see this patch? The one that says if you piss me or my brothers off, no one will ever find your body? I suggest you take a closer look, then back the fuck up and let us through."

His eyes dropped to the Silver Saints patch on my cut, and the color drained from his face. He swallowed hard, then moved to the right, away from the crowd, unblocking the entrance.

"Smart move, dumbass," Grey growled from behind me as we marched into the club.

A bottle blonde in a sparkly outfit that barely qualified as clothes was walking by with a tray. She stopped when she saw us and smiled in a way that made my skin crawl. I was definitely going to need a shower before I went anywhere near my girl again.

"Where is Don Falco?" I demanded.

"Who?" She blinked, trying to appear innocent, but she wasn't a good enough actress to hide the world-weary look in her eyes.

Tired of all the bullshit, I pulled my gun from beneath my jacket and held it at my side, not threatening, but making sure she saw it. "Don. Falco." I enunciated heavily as if talking to a kid.

Suddenly, Nova stood before me, holding out a wad of cash. "Maybe this will jog your memory."

I grunted, frustrated with his tactics even though I knew he had the smarter play.

The woman bit her lip, then shrugged and

snatched the money, tucking it into her bra. "I don't know who you're talking about, but you might find the rooms behind the VIP area more to your liking." She pointed at a roped-off area, then walked off in another direction. I tucked my gun back into place and headed where she'd indicated.

Another bouncer stood in front of the secluded area, but with one look at our cuts and faces, he faked a cough and turned away. Stanchions held up the rope, so I shoved one out of my way and stomped through the darker area with booths where people were doing who the fuck knows what.

A security guy, almost as intimidating as us, guarded a door at the back of the room. When he saw us approaching, he put his finger to his ear and said something. Probably calling for backup.

Since we had no desire to fight unless necessary, I sped up and halted right in front of him, bracing my feet apart and crossing my arms over my chest. "Not here to cause trouble. Tell Falco if he wants McGuire's fifty grand, he'll call off the dogs and let us in."

His gaze moved to the side, and his brow lifted when Dax showed him the black briefcase we'd brought. The guard pressed his finger to his ear again. "Never mind, Hank. Tell the boss someone is here to make a payment."

He listened for a second, then opened the door and moved out of our way.

It was another dimly lit room, but light enough for me to see a small, dark-haired man in a cheap suit sitting in the middle of a half-circle booth. He sat leaning back with his eyes closed, but when we walked in, they opened, and he frowned.

"That's enough, doll," he grunted. "You can finish paying me later."

My lips curled in disgust when another girl, dressed similarly to the first—but much younger. Young enough to turn my stomach if my guess was right—climbed out from under the table and wiped her face with the back of her hand. This douche was centimeters away from eating a bullet.

"Gentlemen. You have money for me?" the man —Don, I assumed—asked.

"Southeast corner," Breaker murmured in my earpiece. "Only man sitting."

He reported our position to Scout, who covered us with a sniper rifle. Since the windows were tinted, Breaker had given him a way to distinguish Falco's heat signature. We all wore a special beacon for him to recognize us, but this way, he'd be able to distinguish the boss from his three henchmen in the room.

"Arthur McGuire. He owes you fifty grand, right?" I clarified.

"Fifty thousand, one hundred and twenty-two dollars and thirty-five cents. To be exact."

I rolled my eyes, and Dax tossed the briefcase onto the table.

"Every penny he owes is in there."

He reached for the cash, and suddenly Nova was at Falco's side, clutching his arm so hard he winced.

"I'm gonna need something in return for collecting your fee," I told him.

"I didn't ask for a bounty hunter," he sneered. "I'll take it out of McGuire's ass."

"Shut the hell up and listen," Nova growled. "If you're smarter than you look, you'll hear him out and hope our favor will be reciprocated."

"Fine," Falco whined. "But let me go."

Nova waited for my nod, then released Falco but didn't move away.

"Once we've cleared Arthur's debt, you agree not to take another bet for him and spread the word that no one is to lend him money or allow him to place bets with them either. Blacklist him."

"And what do I get?"

"Grey here"—I indicated my brother with a jerk of my thumb—"won't make you bankrupt. And Scout"—I pointed at the window behind me—"won't put a bullet in your skull." *Today.*

"You're bluffing," Falco stated, but his eyes were unsure.

"I'm a Silver Saint, motherfucker. I don't bluff."

A shot pierced the glass—without breaking it—and lodged into the leather booth less than an inch from Falco's head.

"What the fuck?" he screamed, scrambling out of the booth. His pants were still unzipped, so his flaccid member flopped out, but he quickly shoved it back in before zipping up his fly.

I'd been sorely tempted to cut it off.

He glanced around for his henchmen, then deflated a little when he realized they wouldn't be any help. My brothers had subdued them with a needle in the neck while Falco had been focused on me and the briefcase.

Grey held up his phone, showing Falco the screen. "That's your account, right? The one that used to have ten grand in it?"

"Used to—what the fuck? Where's my fucking money?" Falco shouted.

"Relax, asshole," Grey grunted. "You'll get it

back when we leave. But if you don't follow through with our favor, you'll be broke in minutes."

"I can't control what other bookies and loan sharks do," he muttered.

"Better figure out a way, Falco," I growled as I grabbed my gun and pointed it at his forehead. "Or you won't have to worry about being broke for long. I'll find you and blow your motherfucking brains out. Understood?"

Falco swallowed, then pressed his thin lips together into a flat line before nodding in defeat. "Now give me my money."

I used the barrel of my weapon to shove the briefcase across the table. Grey tapped a button on his phone, then showed it to Falco again. "Put most of it back," Grey drawled. "Took a son of a bitch tax."

"Fine!" Falco spat. "Now get the hell out of my club."

My brothers and I headed for the back exit, but I stopped and turned around at the last second. "I might need another favor."

Falco glared at me but didn't reply.

"Say I wanted a night with someone…innocent… young…" I was barely able to force the words out.

He stared at me for a long moment, then queried, "How young?"

My eyes flicked to the bottom of the table, and a creepy smile crawled across his face. "If you're willing to pay, I've got *anything* you want."

I forced a conspiratorial smile, then let the door slam behind me after walking out into the back alley.

"Mac?" I asked.

"You have my permission," he growled.

I turned my attention to Grey. "Give him forty-eight hours, then I want him bankrupt and arrested. You can't find enough shit to get him put away, you let me know, and he'll meet with an unfortunate accident."

Grey jerked his chin up in acknowledgment. "Good as done, brother."

The interaction with that fucking sicko had made me feel like I was covered in grime, and I was dying to get home to my woman.

"Dax, Nova," Mac said into our earpieces. "Go see McGuire. Give him the last few thousand and tell him about his new future. Warn him to get his ass in gear and to never, ever touch another woman with force. Phantom, go home."

A part of me felt like confronting Tessa's dad was my obligation, but Mac had given me an order—he'd really given me an out—so I hurried to my motorcycle and drove like a bat outta hell to get back to my Tessa.

I didn't want to face Tessa while I felt so dirty. So I took a long, hot shower in one of the other bathrooms, scrubbing everywhere twice to rid myself of Falco's filth, before returning to my room.

A wide grin spread across my face when I walked in to find Tessa lying on the bed in a green lace teddy that matched her gorgeous eyes.

"You look sexy as fuck, sweet girl," I growled as I shut and locked the door behind me. "But you still disobeyed me, so after I fuck you in all that pretty lace, I'm gonna rip it off and spank your ass until it's cherry red. Then I'm gonna fuck you again while I stare at my handprints on your milky skin."

After I did exactly what I promised, I made love to her, slow and sweet.

"Did everything go okay with the money for my dad?" Tessa asked while we lay wrapped around each other in bed.

"Taken care of."

"Thank you, Kian," she whispered, her jade orbs filled with love as she gazed up at me.

"You know I've got you, sweet girl. Always."

EPILOGUE
TESSA

The family I dreamed of having with Kian happened sooner than either of us expected, thanks to our daughter deciding that she wanted to come three weeks early. She was in such a rush to be born that I almost delivered on the side of the road on the way to the hospital. Luckily, my husband put his excellent driving skills to good use and got us there in the nick of time.

"Damn, that was close." He stroked his finger down our baby girl's little button nose. "I shoulda hauled Patch's ass into the SUV with us, just in case. I won't make that mistake again."

I giggled at the thought of his club brother delivering my baby on the back seat of the vehicle. He was a great doctor who helped out whenever anyone needed it, but he wasn't an OB-GYN. "Nope, our next one will be a boy who listens to his momma instead of our daddy's girl who was in a rush to meet you because you whispered to her about how excited you were for her birth."

"Gonna do the same each time you're pregnant," he warned. "But even if the next one is a momma's boy, I get to name him."

"Absolutely." I wasn't about to argue when he let me name our first after my mom. Honoring her with our little Tabitha was bittersweet since my dad still wasn't a part of my life.

The only updates I got about him were when I asked Kian to check to make sure nothing awful had happened to him. The worst one had been when I learned that he'd sold my childhood home. So many of my happiest memories with my mom had happened there, but Kian had made it better by somehow getting the doorframe where she'd marked my growth each year and cuttings from her rose bushes in the backyard.

Being able to have a part of her in the home where we would raise our family meant the world to me. Even though I had no idea how he'd talked the new owners into it, I wasn't surprised. Kian proved each day how much he meant it when he said he always had my back.

"I love you so much."

"That's good, sweet girl." Carefully cradling our daughter against his broad chest, he leaned over to kiss me. "Because you're stuck with me forever."

"Don't scare the poor girl off," Mac joked as he and Bridget entered the hospital room.

Kian glared at him. "Like you haven't said the same damn thing to your wife."

"He does have a point, dear." Bridget poked Mac in the side before hurrying over to Kian so she could coo at our daughter. "Oh, my goodness. Aren't you so precious? It's hard to believe that ours were ever this small now that they've grown up so much. One of these days, I'm going to blink, and it'll be Molly in that bed after she has our first grandchild."

"Over my dead body," Mac growled. "And whoever the fuck thinks they can knock my little girl up will be six feet under, too."

"Language," Bridget snapped. "The baby is only hours old."

"A little cursing won't hurt her. She's gonna be a Silver Saints princess," he reminded her.

"Well, your first princess just turned sixteen years old, so don't be surprised when we get a call from the school because she thinks she's old enough to use all the swear words she's heard you guys toss around over the years," Bridget muttered, shaking her head with a sigh. "Our girl has enough sass in her that she'd probably make up some of her own just to piss off her teacher and then make a whole case over how she shouldn't be in trouble for using words that don't even make any sense."

I laughed. "I can definitely see her doing something like that."

"Enjoy your precious girl while she's small enough to think that everything you say is gospel," Bridget advised me with a smile. "Eventually, you'll be tearing your hair out over her antics, just like me."

Mac moved closer to his wife and pulled her against his side. "Molly isn't that bad."

"I'm not saying she's bad, just a handful," she corrected. "Which you don't really see because she's a daddy's girl. But some day in the future, she's going to meet a man and she's going to think he's as awesome as you, and then you'll change your tune."

"That's not gonna happen anytime soon since she's not allowed to date until she's at least thirty."

As they continued to banter, Kian leaned close and murmured, "Thirty."

"Thirty what?" I echoed, my brows drawing together.

"That's how old Tabitha will be when she's allowed to go on her first date."

I narrowed my eyes at him. "That's more than a little hypocritical when I got pregnant with her at nineteen."

He shrugged. "Maybe so, but that's the rule."

"Good luck laying down the law with our daddy's girl." I took Tabitha from his arms and smiled down at her. "She's already got you wrapped around her little finger. I bet all it will take is one little pout, and you'll cave. Even when it comes to dating before she's thirty."

He shook his head. "Not gonna happen."

I didn't want to be the kind of person who said I told you so...but I sure as heck did it when he was proven wrong sixteen years later.

EPILOGUE
PHANTOM

"Seriously, Daddy?" Tabitha cried, stomping her foot in frustration.

I folded my arms over my chest and glared right back at her. "Not gonna happen. You're only sixteen."

"Dixon went on a date last week, and he's only fifteen!"

Shrugging, I prepared myself for the tears that would inevitably come soon. "Dixon's a boy. Besides, it wasn't even a real date, Tabby. He went out with a group of friends."

"That's all I want to do. We're going to the dance as a group."

"Boys will get ideas," I argued firmly.

"Aaaargh!" she yelled as she threw her hands in the air. "It's not fair."

"You're my precious baby girl. It's my job to protect you."

Her big blue eyes—so much like my own—filled with moisture, and a fat crocodile tear slipped down her cheek.

Fucking hell.

"I'm growing up, Daddy. You can't protect me forever."

I scoffed. "Watch me."

Her tears began to come in earnest, and I felt a crack in my resolve. My eyes darted down next to me, where my wife sat on the couch, watching me with a smug expression. "You want to back me up on this?"

Tessa shook her head and smirked. "I warned you the day she was born, Kian."

My eyes narrowed, making it clear she would pay for this later.

"I'm not taking her side either."

"That's not gonna save your pretty little ass, sweet girl," I growled, low enough that only she would hear.

"Ewww, Daddy," Tabitha said in a disgusted tone. "Just because I can't hear what you're saying doesn't mean I don't understand. Do you have to do that in front of me?"

"You'll understand when you're older," I murmured with a chuckle.

"Great!" she shrieked happily and ran over to give me a hug before practically skipping out of the room. "Thank you, Daddy!"

"Wait..." I looked back and forth between my daughter and my wife. "What just happened?"

Tessa was laughing too hard to answer at first. I went back over the conversation and still couldn't figure out why she'd suddenly been happy and thanking me.

"You said she'd know when she's older, babe," Tessa explained.

"Yeah...so?"

"She has to date for that to happen."

"What the fuck?" How had she...? I frowned and spun on my heel, ready to storm after my daughter.

"Kian," she said softly, "Let it go, honey. You'll have to get used to the idea of your daughter dating. It might as well be now."

I sighed and glared at the doorway but remained where I was knowing my wife was right. And fucking hating it.

Finally, I slowly turned back around and scowled

at Tessa. "Okay. Let's talk about the fact that you didn't take my side in forbidding my precious baby girl to be around handsy teenage punks."

She rolled her eyes and pushed to her feet. "You've met Grady. He's not stupid enough to be handsy with our girl. No boy in this town would risk your wrath. I was worried no one would ask her to a dance until she was in college."

"And the problem with that is…?"

Tessa patted my chest before walking away. "You've lost this round, babe," she tossed over her shoulder.

Her swaying hips, which had only gotten sexier after having our five kids, stole my attention. Even after seventeen years, my need for her hadn't diminished. It had only grown.

"We'll continue this discussion tonight when the kids are with Rom and Layla," I grunted.

When Tessa winced sitting at the breakfast table the next morning, I was confident I'd made my point.

EPILOGUE
MAVERICK

Birthday party at Silver Saints Clubhouse

I strolled out the back door of the Silver Saints clubhouse into a huge, open space that was hopping with activity since it was a combined birthday party for...who even knew how many kids.

But one of them was my sweet niece, Britta. The second I walked outside, she screamed and came barreling toward me at full speed. I quickly shut the door and crouched down, preparing to catch her. "Hey, button!" I greeted with a laugh when she flung herself into my arms, nearly knocking me over. "Happy birthday!"

She grabbed my hand, and I let her drag me over to my sister, Kansas, who stood next to Grey's old lady, Lorelei. I greeted them with a nod and a smile, then said hello to my sister and kissed her cheek.

Britta tugged on my hand again. "Come play tag, Uncle Mav! Pleeeeeease!"

Callum, another munchkin around Britta's age, ran up and grabbed my other hand. "Yeah, play with us, Uncle Mav!!"

I laughed and shot my sister an amused smile before shrugging. "Lead the way. But don't come crying to your mommas when I kick your butts."

The kids giggled and took off. I waited half a minute to give them a good head start, then took off after them.

"Tag! You're it!" Grayson yelled as he tackled a young woman with long flaming-red hair, who fell to the ground in a heap of laughter.

When she didn't get up right away, I frowned and jogged over to make sure she was okay. I offered her my hand, and when she took it, we locked eyes as I helped her up.

Holy fuck.

She was the most beautiful woman I'd ever seen in my life. Pale creamy skin with a cute sprinkling of freckles, gorgeous emerald eyes, and a body made for sin. Sparks flew from our joined hands, and every nerve in my body lit up like the Fourth of July. Once she was on her feet, we stared at each other, barely aware of the chaos around us.

Suddenly, she poked me in the chest and yelled, "Tag! You're it!" Then she sprinted toward a copse of trees where many of the kids had found hiding spots.

She'd taken me by surprise with her action, but I was still frozen, stunned by my body's reaction. Then Britta tapped my arm, shaking me out of my stupor. "You have to catch her, Uncle Mav."

Catch her? Yes, that was exactly what I needed to do. A wicked smile stole across my face, and I muttered, "I will definitely be fucking catching her." Then I took off in the direction of where my girl had disappeared.

The sun was peeking through the trees enough for me to see the kids darting all around, trying to avoid being caught.

I scanned the area, looking for a sign of the red-headed goddess, but didn't see anything. Then my ears picked up a giggle that was huskier than the others—the laugh of a woman rather than a child.

"Fair warning, baby," I growled as I moved toward the sound. "When I catch you, I'm not going to let you go."

"What makes you think you'll be able to catch me?" she asked, her tone sassy and so fucking sexy it made me rock hard.

I'd spent enough years in the military to know how to be stealthy, so I went into silent mode, slowly stalking my prey.

"Giving up already?" she quipped from about ten feet away.

I grinned when I spotted her perched on a tree branch, searching the area in front of her. As I came up beneath her, I had a spectacular view of her luscious ass. The thought of fucking her from behind, with my handprint on those globes, nearly made me come in my pants.

My hands shot out, and I yanked the branch down, causing her to tumble straight into my arms. She blinked up at me, her emerald orbs filled with shock, and I winked, causing an adorable blush to creep up her cheeks.

"I win," I growled with a devilish smile.

"So it seems, Maverick," she agreed with a smirk.

I raised an eyebrow. "You know my name, so it's only fair that you tell me yours."

"Molly MacKenzie."

I am so fucked...

Curious about the Iron Rogues? Want to know what happens when their VP tries to claim Molly? Find out in Maverick!

In the mood for another age gap romance? If you join our newsletter, we'll send you a FREE ebook copy of The Virgin's Guardian, which was banned on Amazon!

ABOUT THE AUTHOR

The writing duo of Elle Christensen and Rochelle Paige team up under the *USA Today* bestselling Fiona Davenport pen name to bring you sexy, insta-love stories filled with alpha males. If you want a quick & dirty read with a guaranteed happily ever after, then give Fiona Davenport a try!

For all the STEAMY news about Fiona's upcoming releases... sign up for our newsletter!

Printed in Great Britain
by Amazon